THE DAUGHTERS OF POLA

The
DAUGHTERS
of
POLA

FAMILY LETTERS RELATING TO THE PERSECUTION OF DIOCLETIAN FROM AN ISTRIAN MANUSCRIPT

TRANSLATED BY
JOHN MASON NEALE
(OR RATHER, WRITTEN BY HIM)

Arx Publishing
Merchantville, NJ

Originally published by
John Henry and James Parker, London
1861

This edition © 2017 Arx Publishing
Merchantville, NJ

Printed in the United States of America

ISBN 978-1-935228-16-5

"Plures efficimur, quoties metumur a vobis;
semen est sanguis christianorum." *
~Tertullian, *Apologetica,* AD 197

Preface

This is a very curious little book but also a very beautiful one. When originally published in 1861, it did not carry an author's name. In fact, it represented itself as an anonymous translation of an Istrian collection of Latin letters dating from the Great Persecution of Christians under the Roman emperor Diocletian.

Istria, or Histria as it is called in this tale, is a peninsula that juts out into the Adriatic Sea. In our day, it is shared by Croatia, Slovenia, and Italy, but in ancient times, it was near the heart of the Roman Empire. As a result, Roman ruins are plentiful, particularly in the city of Pula—the Pola of the present tale.

The date given at the beginning of the story is AD 303. If you are unfamiliar with this period of history, a little background is in order. In the first two centuries after the Resurrection of Jesus, Christians endured several brutal persecutions. After the persecuting emperor Valerian came to a gruesome end in AD 258— flayed by the King Shapur of Persia following his defeat at the Battle of Edessa—the Church enjoyed forty years of peace.

However, in AD 284, an emperor of the old sort attainted the throne. A native of Dalmatia, a province not far from where the action in *The Daughters of Pola* takes place, Diocletian rose from humble beginnings during the so-called "Crisis of the Third Century." At this time, the Roman Empire very nearly collapsed under pressure from civil strife, barbarian invasion, epidemic plague, and economic instability. A strong military leader and an active administrator, Diocletian is often credited with bringing the empire back from near dissolution, but he is known more infamously as the emperor who presided over the Great Persecution against Christianity. At the instigation of his junior emperor, Galerius, Diocletian issued a series of edicts designed to stamp out the hated followers of the crucified Jew. As recorded by the Christian historian Eusebius Pamphilus who lived through the persecution:

> "It was the nineteenth year of the reign of Diocletian and the month of...March, in

which the festival of our Savior's passion was at hand when the imperial edicts were everywhere published, to tear down the churches to the foundation, and to destroy the sacred Scriptures by fire, and which commanded also that those who were in honorable stations, should be degraded, but those who were freedmen should be deprived of their liberty if they persevered in their adherence to Christianity. The first edict against us was of this nature. But it was not long before other edicts were also issued, in which it was ordered that all the prelates in every place, should first be committed to prison, and then, by every artifice constrained to offer sacrifice to the gods."*

This empire-wide persecution endured for a full eight years. Numerous accounts of the martyrdoms suffered during this tribulation have come down to us in various forms. In their

---

The Ecclesiastical History of Eusebius, 1847, C. F. Cruse (transl.), p. 329.

details, they are similar to the tale told in the present book. This is perhaps not surprising given that the author of *The Daughters of Pola* is John Mason Neale, an outstanding student of patristics and ancient languages.

Neale's familiarity with history and his gifts as a classicist add a wonderful sense of authenticity to *The Daughters of Pola*—absolutely necessary considering he attempted to pass the novel off as a sequence of ancient letters. This pretense adds an overlay of mystery and allows the reader to be immersed completely into the perils of the Christian martyrs. One also gets a sense that Neale was attempting to do more with this tale than simply tell a good story: he was providing a tantalizing doorway to a time long ago, tempting readers into a deeper study of this fascinating historical era.

Lest skeptical modern readers imagine that Neale has merely created a fantasy world from whole cloth in *The Daughters of Pola*, I would encourage them to pick up and read, among others, the authentic passion of Saint Crispina, a Roman Christian matron who was martyred in the year AD 304. Following are a few lines taken from the transcript of her trial before the Roman proconsul Anulinus in Thagara, Africa:

> Anulinus: "Thou shalt lose thy head unless thou wilt observe the commands of the emperor, as they are observed throughout Africa."

> Crispina: "No one shall oblige me to sacrifice to demons. I sacrifice to the Lord only, who made heaven and earth."

Crispina's martyrdom was also mentioned in an extant 5th century sermon by Saint Augustine, and her likeness may be seen to this day among the procession of female martyrs depicted in the apse of the 6th century Basilica of St. Apollinare Nuovo in Ravenna, Italy. So if the Agnella of this tale never existed, we can be confident that real Roman women did suffer publicly for the sake of Jesus Christ with equal courage.

—Anthony P. Schiavo, Jr.
March 2017

Agnella discovered praying.

Introduction

Lloyd's Austrian steamer rounded Point Santa Katherina, and went into the lovely harbor of Pola. Before us rose the three tiers of the amphitheater, of snowy marble, but then reflecting the western rays of a cloudless April evening and arrayed in a vesture of pink like a sunset Alp. White cottage and tall spire gleamed here and there from the thick foliage of the Istrian hills. The peasant drove his oxen—it was Saturday—to their grateful pastures. The vesper bells rang out from the cathedral and from the Island of Saint Katherine. The blue Adriatic was an unbroken sheet of gold. And the "Cheerily, men—oh cheerily!" came from one English vessel weighing anchor.

"Oh, what perfect loveliness and peace!" said I to an Istrian priest who resided in the city and who had come aboard at Rovigno.

"And yet what different associations that amphitheater gives," he replied.

"Truly yes. But yet they seem toned and mellowed down too in the long vista of years."

"I will do myself the honor of taking you over the place, if you will allow me. The *caveae** are remarkably perfect, and some of the seats are marked out, so as to shew how much room each spectator might take. But we have a still more living picture in Pola of the early persecutions."

"How is that?" I asked.

"It is in the temple of Diana, which is now the Museum. There is a large collection of letters, written in the time of Diocletian. I wonder no scholar has edited them."

"What! Christian letters?"

"Christian letters."

"Could you—could any one," I asked eagerly, "get me a sight of them?"

"I will try. We will first see the amphitheater, and then call on the librarian, whom I know well."

And now our vessel blew off her steam. We easily obtained *pratique*, and my new friend and I pulled together to the shore. Marvelous indeed was the amphitheater: seats, holes for

---

Caveae: In a Roman amphitheater, the seating area set aside for spectators.

the awning-supports, Præfect's throne, wild beasts' den, canal, knights' rows, all perfect. The building has this singularity—that in addition to the usual oval, it has four square towers at regular intervals which, it is supposed, were intended for vomitories. Here we talked and fancied and measured till Venus threw her nightly gold-path on the Adriatic.

Not without some difficulty I obtained permission to see the precious records.

They are not, of course, the originals— only copies. There may be fifty in all. I have selected the most important, have endeavored to arrange them in the right order, to give a literal translation of them, and to append a note where necessary.

I hope that they will be as interesting to the reader as they proved to myself. To make them, from the commencement, clearer, I will add a table of the persons by whom they were written.

1. *Diocletian*, Emperor of Rome, residing at Salona.
2. *Marcus Acilius Dolabella*, Præfect of Histria, residing at Pola.

3. *Quintus Flaminius Acerra*, ex-Præfect of Dalmatia, residing at Pomerium, three leagues to the south of Pola.
4. *Justus*, Bishop of Tergeste [Trieste].
5. *Anastasius*, Christian Priest at Pola.
6. *Pythodorus*, a police-officer.
7. *Terentia*, wife to Acilius Dolabella.
8. *Agnella*, daughter to Acilius Dolabella.
9. *Caia*, wife to Flaminius Acerra.
10. *Corellia*, daughter to Flaminius Acerra.
11. *Isiphilus*, an Egyptian Christian, residing at Pola.

The date is AD 303.

I

Quintus Flaminius Acerra, ex-Præfect
of Dalmatia, to Marcus Acilius Dolabella
Præfect of Histria, twice Imperator, Heath.

I lately bought a small statue of Corinthian brass of which the workmanship, I am told, is yet more valuable than the material. It is a Victory and found its way from Athens to Tergeste where my brother saw it and recommended it to my notice. I design it as a gift to the temple of Augustus at Pola. For to whom can such a figure be more appropriately dedicated, than to the eternal Fortune of the Roman Empire? I have given orders for its conveyance to you, and have this further request to make (for I know that nothing which concerns either our own friendship or the worship of the immortal gods can be burdensome to you). My desire, then, is that you would procure a base to be made for it by your best artist, of what marble you please, and will thereon see engraved my name, and (if you think it right) my honors. When I shall hear that this is completed, I will, unless it should be less pleasing to you, pay you a visit for the purpose of inspecting the statue. Farewell.

From Pomerium,
the 6th of the Kalends of May.

II

Marcus Acilius Dolabella, Præfect of Histria, to Q. Flaminius Acerra, ex-Præfect of Dalmatia, Health.

Your Victory, my Flaminius, is indeed a treasure, worthy to be reckoned with

> .... these,
> The works of ancient Scopas,
> Or great Praxiteles:
> The one in living colors,
> The one in glorious stone,
> Inspired to trace the features
> Of God or man alone,

as sweet Horace says. I immediately took counsel with our sculptor, Eratosthenes, a man of merit, and by his advice I chose the marble of Pisinum* for the base. The work is now accomplished, and we propose to place it in the temple on the third day from this time. And in return for so splendid a benefit, this I have to ask, that yourself with your excellent wife and

.... daughter
Fairer than her mother fair,

(O sweet Horace!) would be present at the solemnity of the dedication of this image, at which I myself propose to deliver an oration in praise of the worship of the gods and the goodness of the Emperor in purging the earth from those miscreants who rebelled against their service. I have sent my freedman, Agathodorus, with this epistle, with whom, on his return, I expect a favorable answer. Farewell.

From the Præfectorial Palace,
the 3rd of the Nones of May,
Diocletian VIII, Maximian VII, Consuls.

Pisinum: Mitterburg in German. Now, Pazin in Croatia.

III

Corellia to her sweetest Agnella, Health.

Do you know, darling, that on the Nones, O happiest of days! we are coming to you in town, to assist at the dedication of my father's Victory? I have not seen that dearest of little faces for nearly two months, and I am pining for it again. Let us enjoy as much of each other, sweetest love, as we can. Your Agathodorus takes this.

Hastily, from Pomerium,
the 3rd of the Nones.

IV

Anastasius, Priest, to Justus, Bishop.
Health in the Lord.

You left me in charge, reverend Father, to tell you of each new victim in this persecution, when of a surety it seems as if Antichrist were permitted to exert all his whole strength before the coming of the Lord. I could not, when I last wrote, count more than twenty-six or twenty-seven faithful in this city: libellatics,* as your Paternity knows, in abundance, but apostates hardly any. Since then I have lost two, one by a natural and one by a violent death. Poor old Apollonia, the manumitted slave of the Præfect Acilius Dolabella, who was foster-mother to his daughter Agnella, went home, after a long and grievous illness, yesterday. She had been baptized four years, and it was probably her illness, which confined her so much to her bed, that hindered her faith from being observed. I doubt not that she is with Lazarus in Abraham's bosom, where sorrow and poverty and all ills are ended—and so much concerning her.

The other case is more sad. There was yesterday a grand ceremony here in honor of the dedication of a Victory in the temple of Augustus and of Rome, an image presented by one Flaminius Acerra, living here in the

---

Libellatics: Those Christians who, rather than submit to martyrdom, purchased a fraudulent legal document that said that they had offered sacrifice to the pagan gods. They were termed "libellatics" because they received a "libellus" which was the name of the document.

country. The Præfect delivered an oration in the forum before a very large audience, the winged Victory being set on a kind of table before him, the flamen standing by with the garlanded sheep and oxen ready for the sacrifice. The giver, too, was there with his wife and daughter and the family of the Præfect. It so happened that I was compelled to pass through the forum, on my way home from the death-bed of Apollonia. The Præfect was haranguing on the old stale calumnies against us: the ass's head, the abominable mysteries, the murder of infants—for which God forgive him—when lo, on a sudden there was a hubbub among them that stood nearest the tribunal, and young Roscius Aquilinus, whose father and sister are among the martyrs, and whom I have before now had occasion to rebuke for indiscreet zeal leapt forward. Just as Acilius was boasting of the utter destruction—the pure blotting out, he called it—of the Christian name, Aquilinus cried out, "Præfect, you lie." At the same time he smote the image, which was of Corinthian brass, so mighty a stroke that he broke off the head, which he then spurned with his feet.

The Temple of Augustus in Pola as sketched by Giovanni Battista Piranesi, ca. 1748.

A most horrid uproar arose. The sacrifice was deferred, and Aquilinus was cast into the dungeon. I tried in vain to see him. He was racked last night, even to the seventh hole, all which he bore, as I hear on good testimony, most firmly saying nothing but this, "I have conquered your Victory," "Who will make another head for the poor idol-ling?"* and the like taunts. This morning, being sewn up in a sack with a cock, an ape, and a serpent, he was cast into the Adriatic. So he has conquered. Albeit, I have not so learnt Christ as altogether to praise his deed. Yet, I doubt not that he stands accepted by our Master. Only I fear that his attempt will be the cause of the shedding of more innocent blood still. If I live I will shortly again write to your Paternity. Remember me in the holy Sacrifice, and pray that I may be found ready in the day of the Lord. Farewell.

Hastily, from my accustomed place.

---

* *"Quis de novo caput idolello impotent?"* is the original. —JMN

V

Corellia to her Agnella, Health.

The disturbance occasioned by that Christian miscreant prevented me, dearest one, from seeing so much of my darling as I had hoped. But this one thing I saw, or thought I saw, that something was on her mind which she would not let me share. Have we not, darling, been friends before we can recollect? And shall we not trust each other now? If there is anything that I can do, or say, or ask, for my poor little lamb, tell me, and I will be a faithful shepherdess. My father, as you may well believe, is more full of rage against that scum than ever. Insolent malefactor! But write to me, and that soon, and tell me what is the matter with that tender little heart, and trust it to my love to find a remedy. Farewell.

From Pomerium,
the 4th of the Ides of May.

VI

Agnella to her Corellia, Health.

It is very true, my heart, only I did not mean that you or that any one else should have discovered it. It is very true that I have been and am still, grievously unhappy. The cause, if I could tell any one, I could tell you, but yet not without your assurance that you will keep my secret—a very different one from any that you imagine, or that we in our girlish days may have talked about. Give me your word only to keep inviolably that which I shall trust you with, and it will be a comfort to me greater than I can describe to let you know all. Farewell.

From the Præfectorial Palace,
the 12th of the Kalends of June.

VII

*Marcus Acilius Dolabella, Præfect of Histria,
to Quintus Flaminius Acerra, ex-Præfect of
Dalmatia, Health.*

At length, my Flaminius, the Victory has
been placed in the temple of Augustus.
The sacrilegious wretch who so profanely
violated it has paid, as you know, the penalty
of his crime, but not alone. I had not believed
that another Christian existed in this city, but
by diligent enquiry I discovered two whom,
after I had put to the torture, I caused to be
thrown into the Adriatic. But there is another
matter in which I would ask for your help. My
wife has noticed—for truth to say, I am not
myself observant of such matters—that my
Agnella has since your departure been much
given to melancholy and loneliness, than
which nothing is more contrary to her nature.
We consulted my freedman Epaminondas,
a physician, and being unable by the art
of medicine to assign any cause for such
melancholy of spirit, he attributes it rather
to a visitation of Pan. Hence, four days ago,

I sacrificed four black sheep to that god. But either we are in the old age of the world when the divinities will cease to hear prayer, or such is our wickedness that we have no longer access to their mercy. For from that time, my daughter, instead of making progress, has been sensibly, and that day by day, worse. Epaminondas now says that perchance a change of scene would do her good. For that the lymphatic portion of her vital powers might thereby be restored to their natural tone, and she might become herself again. Can you then, and your excellent Caia, receive her for a few days at Pomerium? She, I think, will be well pleased to make the journey and again to be in the society of her dear Corellia. Farewell.

From the Palace,
the 12th of the Kalends of June,
Diocletian the eighth time,
Maximian the seventh time, Consuls.

VIII

Corellia to her dearest Agnella, Health.

Write to me what you will, my little heart, only write speedily and with all truth. Pylades was never so true to Orestes as I will be to you, and never believe the stupid old philosophers who say that a woman cannot keep a secret. Farewell.

From Pomerium,
the 11th of the Kalends of June.

IX

Agnella to her darling Corellia, Health.

I have just heard from my father—O happy tidings!—that I am to spend some time with you, and that we set forth on the 7th of the Kalends. But I had rather tell you my secret by letter than by word of mouth: for indeed, by word, I do not think that I could summon courage to speak it.

You have heard me talk to you of my poor old nurse, Apollonia, the same who, while you were with me, went to the More. She had been ill for four months. Several times I saw her in her illness, and ever I marvelled at her great patience, and, I had almost said, happiness. In such miserable, worn-out, poor old age, it seemed to me little less than magic that she should always be so cheerful, so grateful for any little present, so ready to hear every matter about her old family, quite forgetting her own sufferings, even as if they were those of a stranger. I often asked her how she could so bear up under her sorrow, but never could get any other answer than this, "You shall know before I die." Once I saw in her room, though but for one moment, a most pleasing old man, so gentle, so friendly, who seemed to be comforting her to his best of power. I asked who he was, and still the same answer—"You shall know, lady, before I die." Two days, —now it comes, darling. Do not hate me, pet. Do not despise me—two days before you came, I went again to her miserable room, leaving Agathodorus below. She was stretched, as usual, on her wretched sack, a bundle of straw forming her pillow, and now clearly near death, her poor hands folded on her breast, her breath laboring, and by her side was this good man.

"Oh nurse!" I said, and I could not help bursting into tears.

"Do not weep for me, little lamb," she replied; "and I will tell you why not. But if I do, will you keep my secret till the breath is out of my body?"

"Surely, dear nurse, I will."

"You may trust her, father. Now read to her and to me once more the story about—" I did not catch the name.

In a very sweet voice, but with a slightly foreign accent, he read a most lovely story about a beggar who lay at a rich man's gate, himself full of sores and desiring to be fed with the crumbs that fell from that man's table; how the dogs licked his sores; how then he died. You will say, "Nothing much in that. What then?" He went on to say that he was carried by messengers into the bosom of one of the gods, and how the rich man died and was buried, and woke up in Tartarus, and there asked for one drop of water to cool his tongue, and there was none to give it him, and how the poor beggar was comforted, but he tormented.

"Who wrote that?" I asked.

The old man paused a moment, and then said, " Christ."

Then it flashed on me that they were Christians.

"Oh, nurse, nurse! How can you? How can you? Oh, what will become of you and of me?"

"Become of me?" she said. "Why, by God's goodness, in a few hours I shall be where that poor beggar now is. And there, sweet lamb, I want you to be."

"Never! Never! Worship an ass's head? Never!"

"My child," said the old man, "someday you will learn, I hope, that we do none of these wicked things that are imputed to us, that we worship none but God and His only Son, our Lord, with Whom your dear nurse is soon going to live."

I could not help being struck by his words, and could only cry.

"Come nearer to me, darling. Pet, this is what I have always meant to tell you, and to ask you before I go. You have wondered that I should be so happy. You knew the worship of your gods could not make me so, but because I put my whole trust in Jesus Christ—"

"But He was a crucified wretch," said I.

"Father, forgive her," said the old man, very softly, "she knows not what she says."

"He *was* crucified," said Apollonia. "He bore all I bear, and a thousand-fold more, and for that very reason I love Him and trust Him, and shall soon, I hope, be with Him. Father, you will pray for her ?"

"I will," he said.

"How long have you been a Christian, nurse?"

"Four years."

Then came on a paroxysm of hard breathing, and I thought she was going. But she recovered, and then said, "Now you must not stay, and you will not see me again. But I hope you will see the priest."

"No, no," I answered.

"I hope so, and if of His goodness I ever enter into rest, I will not cease to pray for you. I must not trust you with his dwelling, but—"

"But, lady," said he, "if God shall touch your heart and you ever do desire to see me, you have but to leave a written message in this very room. I know I am putting myself somewhat in your power, but I believe that I may trust you. At all events, I will trust you, and I am sure that, at least while your nurse lives, you will do nothing which could injure her."

"So far I promise you," I said, "for though I hate your religion and hate Christ, you shall never have to complain that I betrayed any one who put confidence in me." And so I bade Apollonia farewell, and went home with Agathodorus. Somehow, what I had seen made a great impression on me, even while you were there, and more so when I heard that the poor thing was dead. I could not help particularly remembering the story of the beggar that was carried by the messengers into the bosom of the gods. But since you have left us, something much more wonderful has happened. First I must tell you how it began.

My father had given a great supper at the new *stibadium** which you admired. As he

---

A kind of horseshoe table much in fashion in the third and fourth centuries. —JMN generally wishes, I was there, and sat between him and Marcus Terentius, who has come over here on some business from the Augustus. It was a long tedious business—from the eggs to the apples must have been at least four hours—and there was a stupid poet who stood at the bottom of the table and read a panegyric on my father, and had some of the broken meat given him afterwards. Well, at last it was over, and I was very glad to find myself in my own room that looks into the garden, and to send Glycerium away when she had let down my tower. I sat down before the window that you and I have so often looked out of. It was a dark night, a soft, hazy, perfumed, spring night, everything was quite quiet, except the croaking of frogs a long way off. And the night breeze brought in all the thousand scents of our garden, and blew so pleasantly on me after the heat and turmoil of our party. I know not how long I had been looking out of the window at nothing. My lamp burnt out, and

---

*The tower was a particular way of doing the hair, especially fashionable under the later emperors, which raised it up to a great height, and padded it out into the resemblance of a building. It sometimes took three hours to complete. —JMN

still I sat on, thinking in a dreamy way of our banquet, and the mullet that my father had been vexed with, because it died directly after it was set on the table, and the rich man that went to Tartarus, and the dogs that licked the poor beggar's sores. Well, all on a sudden (I cannot tell you how I could see in the dark, but so it was) Apollonia seemed to stand between me and the window. It was she, and yet it was not. The features were the same, only so much younger, and so beautiful, and she was dressed, not in the rags in which I last saw her, nor yet in the nurse-fashion in which I can remember her when I was a child, but in a most glorious white garment, which shone as if it were gold. And she had the sweetest smile on her lips that I ever saw, and either she said, or I fancied it, "I told you I would pray for you, and I have." And then it was all dark again.

You will think, my darling, that I must have lost my senses, and sometimes I think so myself. But yet I cannot tell you how this comes back and back upon me. I am sure that you will keep what I have written a secret, for my father would be grievously angry if he thought that I had had any communication with those Christians. But to go on, there was no sleep for me that night. I had a great mind to call back Glycerium, only I did not well know what excuse to make for asking her to stay with me, and so I lay hour after hour till after daybreak. The next morning, my father enquired, as well he might, if I were ill. And that was the beginning, I think, of his wanting to send me to you. Now before I leave home, let me have one little letter, just to say that you do not think me mad and that you do not love me the less. Farewell.

From Pola,
the 9th of the Kalends.

X

Corellia to her Agnella, Health.

Love you the less? No, never! I only pity you the more, that you should have fallen into the influence of that miserable and lost set. But it will pass, dearest, it will pass. Yes! Wiser heads than yours, you stupid little Agnella, have been entangled by it for a time. However, come to me as you are coming and I will tell you plenty of stories that will make you laugh, and some that will make you shudder, about these people. Two years ago my father, when he was Præfect of Dalmatia, condemned a deacon, as they call them, to the scorpions. And when that torture forced him to speak the truth, he confessed that, every Sabbath morning, he and his fellows were accustomed to drink the blood of infants out of silver vessels. I cannot quite fancy my Agnella drinking the blood of infants, nor yet keeping Sabbaths like those filthy circumcised Jews. You knew that you might trust me, and not a word of this shall ever pass my lips, but I am very glad that you are coming. Farewell.

From Pomerium,
the 7th of the Kalends.

XI

Marcus Acilius Dolabella, Præfect of Histria,
to Pythodorus, Health.

I am informed, my Pythodorus, that whereas we had imagined the execrable sect to be at an end, they are indeed gathering fresh courage and exerting themselves to make new converts in this place. I have this day heard some strange report concerning that Apollonia who was once nurse in my family. I give it you in charge, then, to learn what you can of those who visited her in her last illness, and to discover in what religion she died. Farewell.

From Pola,
the 7th of the Kalends.

XII

Agnella to Corellia, Health.

It seems, dearest friend, that my father, who had intended to accompany me to

Pomerium, is prevented by magisterial business, and he has just asked me whether I would rather defer my journey for some days yet till he can go with me, or whether I should prefer to start at once with Agathodorus for my companion. To tell you the truth, Corellia, I feel fitter at this present moment for my own company than for any one's else, even yours. Whatever you say, whatever I hear said by my father, I cannot but believe that there is more in this religion than we yet imagine. Anyhow, was it not the strangest of all strange things that my poor old nurse, surrounded as she was with everything miserable, pain and poverty, and the certainty of death, should yet be so happy? Did you ever know any of our poor that were? And this puzzles me above all things: why men should so willingly and joyfully die for a falsehood, whereas none of us would die for what we hold to be truth.

You say that one man confessed about the blood of infants, but how many have I myself seen tortured who constantly denied those things with their latest breath! If I could, I would for myself procure some of their sacred books, but I know not well how to set about it. Of this I am certain: that one way or the other, I will have more assurance, and that I shall never find rest till I have either heard what some Christian has to say for himself, or read their writings. In the meantime, you must not be angry with me but rather pity me, for I would give anything not to have seen poor Apollonia, and so to have remained contented as, till now, I have been.

By the time we meet, I hope that my difficulties will be set at rest. Farewell.

From Pola,
the Kalends of July.

XIII

Anastasius to Justus, Bishop,
Health in the Author of Health.

Verily holy Father, now as ever, *sanguis martyrum, semen Ecclesiæ.**

---

*English translation: "The blood of the martyrs is the seed of the Church." This is a common paraphrase of Tertullian's quote featured at the beginning of this book.

I told your Paternity not long since of the happy departure of one Apollonia, foster-nurse in the family of Acilius Dolabella, now Præfect. I did not, I think, add that the daughter of the said Acilius, who had many times visited her nurse in her illness, came just before her death when I was in the sick room and learnt that we were Christians. And Apollonia, whether of mere natural hope or by a certain prophetic instinct which I have often noticed to accompany the dying, told her foster-child with many tears that if ever she herself should be dissatisfied with the worship of idols, she needed but to leave a line there in that cottage and I would answer it. Then followed the destruction of the Victory and, as I foretold your Paternity would be the case, a sharper enquiry after Christians. We have two more among the martyrs: Epitherses, by trade a druggist, who (the report goes) was poisoned with viper's theriac; and Palmella, a girl aged sixteen, who was first exposed in the *lupanaria* and thence marvelously delivered by the Angel of the Lord and so beheaded at the Tergestean gate. They affirm that at the time and very moment of her victory a white dove was seen to soar away to heaven.

But now comes the marvel.

In that very room where Apollonia dwelt, lives one Isiphilus, an Egyptian by birth, long since a Christian. Him, very infirm with old age and many maladies, I oftentimes visit. When I went to him two days agone he said, after salutations, "Here is a note which was left for you last evening by a woman that desired not to be known." I took it and therein read—"I remind you of a promise made by a deathbed to one who is now very unhappy and who desires to see you."

It were tedious to tell you how after some long series of difficulty I, at length, found means to appoint a meeting with Agnella (for such is her name and the Lord of the fold grant her to be a true lamb therein!). But so I did, and two days since, I met her in the very same room in which Apollonia had departed to the joy of her Lord. She came, closely veiled, by herself. I advanced as she entered, but without noticing me, she threw herself in the chair provided for her, leant over the table, and hid her face in her hands. I waited till her first burst of grief should pass, for she was sobbing violently.

At length I said, "My child, you could not have thus summoned the priest of a poor despised sect unless it had pleased God to touch your heart. Tell me what is your doubt or grief, and as our Lord shall give me wisdom, believe me that I will do all I can to help you."

Now she looked up, stilled herself with an effort, and threw her veil back. She was, I guessed, about eighteen years old, and there was a kind of quiet placidity in the general tone of her countenance, as I by degrees perceived, which would have led me to imagine her a Christian already. Very beautiful she is, and that also will be a greater difficulty in her way, for with such riches and so much beauty, it is not likely that Satan should easily allow his prey to be taken from him.

"I am unhappy. Oh, I am unhappy indeed!" and then another burst of tears.

"It was to the unhappy that my Lord came, and that I am sent. But if I am to be made the means of giving you comfort, I must first—must I not?—know the cause of your sorrow."

"You remember when I was here before?"

"Most perfectly."

"And what I saw then?"

"I shall never forget it."

"I marvelled then at the quietness and peace and hope in which Apollonia could die. It made an impression on me that I could not account for. But since then—"

"Well, since then?"—for she hesitated.

"You will not believe me if I tell you."

"I see you to be most deeply in earnest. I will believe you fully."

Then she told me how one evening after a banquet given by her father, in the silence and darkness of her own chamber, she beheld the same Apollonia in glory. How could I but worship and adore the God Who doeth wonders?

"What does this mean?"

"It means, my child, that our Lord would have you His own. It means that He has permitted you to see your dear foster-nurse as she is. Tread in her steps and you shall be like her."

"Oh, if I could but believe your faith! For I know not what I believe or rather if I believe anything at all. I have sometimes felt that I could worship the God of Majesty when we have done sacrifice to Jupiter, and the God of Beauty when we have adored Phœbus, but some rites—some rites," and her cheeks and neck *burnt* with the blush that overspread them.

"You mean," I said, "that some rites, so far from seeming to you worthy of beings of perfect goodness and blessedness, like the immortal gods, are such as it shames and vexes and pains you to remember even now."

"It is so indeed."

"And you mean most of all, I suppose, those rites of the Grecian temple to Aphrodite in which, as I heard, you took a part."

No answer, except a deeper blush.

"And *could* those be gods? He Who *is* God, Who made heaven and earth, Who shall come hereafter to judge the quick and the dead, He is the God of purity also. Myself was once a slave to these vanities. I have also known the abominations of which you speak. And now tell me what it is that has brought you here? For you must yourself know that such a conversation as this would be perilous, even for you."

Then she told me—and marvellous it is to see how, as saith the blessed Apostle of the Gentiles, "God hath mercy on whom He will have mercy." It was not the vision alone, though that was the crowning point, but it was the long course of events before which led her to receive the messenger more readily. I could perceive that for months past, the God Whom she knew not had been drawing her to Himself, had been giving her the desire of a firm true standing-ground that could not be moved, and had filled her with unutterable loathing towards those impure mysteries which other Roman women either care not for or love.

At that time we talked for about two hours, and I do not mean to say that all her difficulties, nay, that the half of them, were removed. The fables of the ass's head and the infants' blood I think she no longer regards, but her stumblingblock, as of old, is a suffering God. Yet, as blessed Paul quoted Aratus and Menander, so did I also to this poor child, who has been well brought up in Greek learning, quote Sophocles, that noble passage at the end of the *Philoctetes*,* where Hercules tells how

---

Philoctetes by Sophocles (written ca. 410 BC) contains a line spoken by the ghost of Herakles: "Thou too like me by toils must rise to glory—Thou too must suffer, ere thou canst be happy."

no true glory can be won save by suffering.

How this matter will end, God only knows. On the sixth day we are to meet again but then at Pomerium. There she goes on a visit to the ex-Præfect of Dalmatia, and there I also have to comfort three or four Christians scattered in a land of darkness and of the shadow of death.

I could perceive also that both the death of Palmella, but more especially her exposure to the insults of wicked men and the deliverance wrought for her by the Angel of the Lord, dwelt much on the mind of Agnella whom I doubt not our Lord will, in His good season, receive into His fold. To which end, holy Father, I desire both your prayers and the sacrifice of the Immaculate Lamb. Farewell.

From my appointed place,
at this time.

XIV

Diocletianus, Emperor, Consul for the eighth time, to Marcus Acilius Dolabella, Præfect of Histria, twice Imperator, Health.

I have always, my Acilius, praised your zeal in the hunting out and bringing to condign punishment those execrable miscreants who bear the name of Christ. The more, therefore, am I grieved—for I would not willingly to so tried a friend say *angry*—at the horrid sacrilege which, as it is here reported, was lately perpetrated at Pola. For they affirm that a dedicated Victory was, by some Tartarean evil-doer, broken up and spurned on the ground. Of this, and of the afore said miscreant's punishment, you will forthwith render me the strictest account. Farewell.

From my palace at Salona,
the 10th of the Ides of July,
myself the eighth time,
Maximianus the seventh time, Consuls.

XV

Agnella to her own Corellia, Health.

You will listen, dearest friend, with
patience, even if you cannot approve.
Someday, perchance, we shall think more
alike. I have seen—it may as well be told
now as at any other time—a Christian priest,
and when I am forced to own how utterly I
have been deceived in many matters, I can
more than half believe that I may be wrong
in all. But I could not bear up against my
desire to know more of these men and their
doctrine, and so not without difficulty, I left
a short epistle at Apollonia's house earnestly
entreating to see the priest for myself. So, not
to weary you, at last I did see him. Oh, how
gentle he was! Oh, how he appeared to know
a truer and better life than any that we can
imagine in this world!

About the vision he seemed not at all
astonished. He only said, "Our God is the
God Who doeth wonders, and thus He would
lead you to Himself." But when I thought how
in every way we have persecuted, abused,

ridiculed these poor people, leaving them neither home nor hope, and then saw how entirely they forgive us, saying that in truth they have nothing to forgive, for that we only send them to their true home by a speedier journey, Corellia, I feel sure that they have the right on their side!

Yet I have many difficulties still, but we are to meet again. He constantly denies that they worship anything made with human hands, but only the great God and His Son Jesus Christ, and that to Him they daily offer a sacrifice, of which he refused to tell me till I shall have been initiated in their first mysteries. Do not misunderstand me, as yet I have not made up my mind to this. Certainly I shall go no further till I have seen you, which will be on the day that follows my next visit to him. One thing that he said to me very much surprised me. He said that all knowledge of truth must be the gift of God, and only to be gained from Him by earnest prayer. "Pray," he said, "to our God, if you have faith to believe that He exists. But, at all events, pray to whatever deity your own heart does acknowledge, and the God Whom you ignorantly worship will hear you."

And this again struck me much, that he should make so much of my praying to the gods. When did a flamen ever tell me so? I feel in my own conscience that so far he is right, and also I feel that he alone, of all priests I ever saw, understands that feeling of guilt and fear of the vengeance of the gods which a hecatomb of oxen could never remove. There is something in his religion which speaks to my heart. I can tell you better when we meet. Only, since Agathodorus is setting forth for Pomerium this day, I thought best to write thus much without loss of time. Farewell, and love me ever.

From Pola,
the 3rd of the Ides of July.

XVI

Pythodorus to Marcus Acilius Dolabella, Health.

The letters which I received from your Splendor should have found a more speedy reply, had it not been for certain difficulties appertaining to the subject into which you commanded me to enquire. I have, however, made every inquisition into the circumstances attending the deathbed of your late manumitted slave, by whom she was attended, in what religion she professed herself to die, who were they that visited her, and who accompanied her burial. Your Splendor knows well that during the twenty-three years I have held my post as police-officer in this city, I have never been found wanting either in the investigation of offenses or in the punishment of offenders. But now, I confess, I would advise that no further enquiry be made into this matter. I have reasons which may safely remain in my breast, but which would with less convenience be entrusted to another. And so, commending you to the care of the immortal gods, I pray you to accept of my service. Farewell.

From Pola,
the 12th of the Kalends.

XVII

Marcus Acilius Dolabella to Quintus Flaminius Acerra, Health.

Either, my Acerra, the world is in its old age and all things, as the philosophers tell us, are returning to imbecility, or those persons with whom I was wont to act in my political relation are be coming mad. I had desired Pythodorus, who I think is known to you no less than to myself, as an active magistrate of police, to make enquiry as to the deathbed of my manumitted slave of whom we conversed. This is his answer.

What do you advise me to do? Is it possible that the dog should be a member of that execrable sect himself (for you know my fears) or that he should speak in the real interest of the emperor, and that here are matters into which, for the sake of the republic, I had better not enquire? Whatever be your opinion, write me word speedily, for the matter will hardly brook delay. I trust that your more favorable climate will speedily improve my daughter's health. To her I send the love of a father, and to your wife and daughter all good greetings and wishes. Farewell.

From the Præfectorial Palace at Pola, the 11th of the Kalends.

XVIII

Anastasius, Priest, to Justus, Bishop, Health in the Author of Health.

Y ou, who have so often and so well known, most reverend Father, how according to that saying of blessed Paul, the grace of God makes use of things that are not, either to bring to nought or to bring to happiness things that are, will perhaps marvel less than my weaker faith wonders, when you hear that Agnella, the daughter of our Præfect, has given her name to Christ. Praise, therefore, be to Him That doeth wonders.

But, as you instructed me with all diligence to make known to you whatever should happen in these parts, I will relate to you that which has happened since, now three days

The Arch of the Sergii in Pola, originally one of the city gates, as sketched by Giovanni Battista Piranesi, ca. 1748.

agone, I left Pola. And no such easy matter is it to leave that city, since for the last three months the gates have been strictly watched on the landward side, and none can go into the country without the Governor's pass. Hiring, therefore, a boat from one Athenodorus, who though a libellatic, yet purposes when the persecution is over to be put in penance, I set sail with him and with another, under color as though we were about to take palamydes in the bay.

That night, not without danger, running along the coast in the grey of the morning, we cast anchor in the port of the Palm about half a league from Pomerium. Here, as I told your Fatherliness, I had one or two scattered sheep of my flock to visit, and principally the widow Olympia whose husband died for Christ in the last persecution and who herself, through the torments she then endured, has since lost the use of the left arm—a glorious proof of her confessorship.

Creeping in secretly there on a rainy morning, I took counsel with Olympia in what way I might most easily come to speak with her whom I principally came to seek. And herein God opened a path beyond my hopes. The brother of Olympia, by name Stasimus (for they are Greeks) a heathen, indeed, but yet a kind man by nature and within reasonable limits to be trusted, dwells near to her. He is a worker in Histrian marble, and the pedestal of a certain Mercury that stands in the porticus of Acerra being broken, he was employed to mend it. It was now finished, and he being over-busy with his trade, thankfully accepted his sister's offer to carry up the thing (it was but small) to the villa. Thus she had speech of Agnella and came back full of joy.

"God be praised, father," said the good motherly woman, "that you are here. She longs to see you, I am sure all will go well. She cannot fix an hour, but come she will, and that at whatever cost, within two days. Only you must be ready to receive her day or night."

In the grey of the next morning, while I was yet sleeping, I heard the voice of my hostess, "She is here, father." I rose in a moment, and going into the little cottage room—living and kitchen room in one—behold, there was Agnella. At first I thought she had fainted. But, by an effort, she speedily recovered herself.

"What have I done? What have I done?" she cried. "Oh, father, do not deceive me! I am too miserable to argue. I would only try to believe. Are you sure—are you sure with all your heart and soul, that this Jesus whom I have been taught to hate and to ridicule, is indeed Lord and God?"

"What else, my child, could carry us through what you know that we suffer? What else could have filled your dear nurse, in the midst of all her poverty, all her misery, all her disease, with such unspeakable joy? That one case you yourself saw, but I could tell you of a hundred more such as that. You tell me that your belief never could satisfy the love and faith and hope of your mind. There was no foundation, no certainty—"

"You say it," she interrupted, "as if you could read my heart."

"Because I can read your heart, my poor child, because I have had the sorrows and doubts of many and many such a heart laid open to me before this—sorrows and doubts that have now long since ended in peace and certainty."

And so, step by step, I set before her the

great mysteries of our faith, more clearly than ever as yet. I felt, even as I spoke, that it was no power of my own, that it was no cogency of my arguments, which was convincing her mind. The Lord Himself was almost visibly on my side, and the grace of the great God the Comforter shone more and more certainly into that poor, dark, bereaved, bewildered mind.

At last—"Never yet," she said, "have I been able to pray to the God Whom you worship, but now, if I might, I could. Will you pray to Him with me, and for me, now?"

So we knelt down on that cottage floor, and while the neighboring pine-groves sang their sweet and solemn anthem to God, there went up to heaven the first earnest cry from another of the souls redeemed by Calvary. She earnestly sought for baptism then and there, yet I thought not good at once to listen to her request. For her there seemed no especial reason for haste, and if I should be taken from the world, I promised her that I would make the case known to you, so that care would still be taken that her regeneration were not too long deferred. In the meanwhile I told her that in one month from that time, all things favoring it, she should enter the salutary laver, and I gave her a little parchment of instructions and prayers, only beseeching her to guard them with all care.

It is not that I myself doubt her stability, but that this I think the part of a Christian priest, not to take advantage of any impulsive feeling, especially in one of her sex and age, and rather to run the risk of her relapsing as a catechumen than to incur the least possible peril of her becoming an apostate.

Meanwhile, I commend both this lamb and myself to your Holiness's prayers, for I know of how great weight they are with God. Farewell.

From my place at this time.

XIX

Justus, Bishop, to Agnella, Catechumen, Increase of Grace in the Author of Grace.

I have heard, beloved child, and that not without joy unspeakable, that it has pleased God, the giver of all good things, to call you to the knowledge of His eternal truth. And I pray that He may give you perseverance to the end and, after all the troubles of this miserable and haughty world, a happy entrance into His everlasting kingdom. And I will not cease to pray for you, that you may be so carried through the temptations of this evil age, as that the white robe which you are so soon to assume you may carry spotless to the end. Farewell.

From Tergeste,
the Kalends of Sextilis.

XX

Corellia to her Agnella, Health.

Words cannot express to you, darling lamb, how again and again and again have I myself enquired of Olympia if she had any letter for me. As the gods would have it, my father and mother have been much absent from home, and therefore I could, with the less suspicion, make my way by that dark pine-wood where you, my pet, and I have more than once walked. But now they have returned, and I must be on my guard lest I should draw their attention to that poor old widow.

It is hard work, this waiting. But I am sure that my Agnella will not forget her promise, and that as soon as there is anything to be told, I shall hear. For myself, I am as I was. I can not believe, I cannot wish to believe, that all we have ever been taught is a lie—that our priests are only deceivers, that there is no such thing as faith. At least our poor believe, and that nurse of yours—poor old dame! How well I remember her, before either you or I had offered our hair to Venus!—would have worshipped our gods just as devoutly as (you tell me) she did your Christ. But those dear little lips of yours have such a pretty way of putting things that, Jupiter love me! I can sometimes hardly resist you when you are with me. Write however. Write soon and write truly. Farewell.

From Pomerium,
the 4th of the Ides of Sextilis.

XXI

Agnella to her own Corellia, Health.

I thought, sweetest darling, that you would be anxious for further intelligence regarding your own once loved—yes, and as I hope still loved—friend. But it was not easy to carry out that on which my heart's desires were bent, and also difficult to find a safe messenger who might deliver this letter to Olympia.

But I can now trust the bearer, and I trust you, the companion of my youth. And above all, I trust the God whom we Christians worship, and His only Son, Jesus Christ our Lord.

Twice in the course of the month that he had appointed, I heard from—and once I saw—the Priest Anastasius. And finally, four days agone, I was received into the Christian Church.

I must not tell you where it was, but at day-break I met the Priest in the appointed place, and he led me into the little church of the Christians here. It is situated underground, in an outskirt of the city, the entrance from a bathhouse in a suburban villa. It was still dark, as together we went to the spot, but yet while in the city, we walked separately for fear of falling in with someone to whom I might be known. Then, as we turned off from the high-road, he waited till I came up with him, and spoke so comfortably of that better hope which is laid up for us, and of the necessity that we must suffer in this life if we would reign in the next, that my very heart burnt within me, and I felt as if all danger and trouble and misery were for Christ's sake to be desired and fondly embraced. We went into the bath-house, the door being opened to a special kind of knock, a grave-looking old man with a sweet countenance said to me, "Welcome, in the Name of the Lord!"

Down the staircase we went, and entered the church. Very small and poor it was: a few lamps burning here and there, a kind of altar at the farther end, with a cross standing on it, a few men to the left hand, a few women to the right. I knew none but Isiphilus. They all rose.

The Priest said, "I bring a new subject of Jesus Christ. Who will be her undertaker and sponsor?"

Then there rose a lady, whom I knew not,

with a very sweet face, and said, "I will, if our new sister will accept of me."

"Eusebia, then, shall be your sponsor," said the Priest. And I thanked her with all my heart.

But, oh, friend and dear companion of my childhood, how that heart beat! How even then I could almost have drawn back! How I shrunk from the final separation that should part my family and myself forever and ever!

I should have told you that near the end of the church where we entered, there was a marble pool filled with water as clear as crystal. A flight of steps descended into it. And now the Deaconess of the church, Octavia by name—she seemed about thirty years of age, and wore a dark palla, somewhat like a widow's—came forward, and Anastasius asked, "Are all things ready?"

"They are," she said, "my father."

"Then the Deaconess Octavia," said the Priest, "will prepare you for the life-giving Sacrament."

She took my hand with a sweet smile, and led me into a little closet adjoining the pool. Here she undressed me, taking off also every single ornament I wore, and letting down my hair. Then she put on me a long white garment, and kissing me, led me forth barefoot to the little assembly. The Priest, meanwhile, had also put on a white robe, somewhat like that of a flamen of Jupiter.

He made me stand facing the west then, and renounce the Evil One and his works. He signed me with the Cross, breathed on me, bade the evil spirit depart, and then Octavia led me to the pool, giving me her hand down the steps, but not descending with me. The water rose even to my shoulders.

Then the Priest said, "Dost thou believe in God the Father Almighty?"

I answered, "I believe."

"And in His only Son?"

"I believe."

"And in the Holy Ghost?"

"I believe."

"And in the Catholic Church?"

"I believe."

"And in the forgiveness of all sins?"

"I believe."

Then, out of a silver vessel he poured water thence on my head, saying, "Agnella, I baptize thee in the Name of the Father, and of the Son, and of the Holy Ghost, now and ever, and to ages of ages. Amen."

And after that, when I had been again dressed in my own clothes, they gave me honey to eat. And first Eusebia, and then the other women, came forward in turn and gave me the kiss of peace.

Oh, Corellia! How happy, notwithstanding all my doubts and fears and uncertainties, I am! Oh, what a different thing is life now from that which it was in the days of my ignorance! Oh, that God may someday bring you, dearest one, into the same hope and bind us together in one and the same love! Farewell.

From Pola,
the 10th of the Kalends of September.

XXII

*Diocletianus, Emperor, for the eighth time
Consul, to Marcus Acilius Dolabella,
Præfect of Histria, Health.*

Albeit, my Acilius, that you have made good every part of a true citizen and of a zealous man in tracing out and punishing the horrible sacrilege of which you write, yet it appears to me that there must be an undercurrent of ill-feeling towards the immortal gods, of which this enormity was only one expression and (so to speak) vent. And whereas none is exempt from the care of celestial worship, I myself propose to visit your province some ten days hence, and should any miscreants of the Christian superstition be before that time brought before you, I desire that they may be reserved to my own hearing. Farewell.

*From Salona,
the 9th of the Kalends of September,
myself the eighth time,
Maximian the seventh time, Consuls.*

XXIII

Pythodorus to Marcus Acilius Dolabella,
Præfect of Histria, Health.

Since it is your will to be made acquainted with the result of my enquiries regarding the death of your manumitted slave Apollonia, I will set it down in brief here:

I find that she died in the Christian irreligion, having been visited in her last illness by one Justus, who is reported to be the bishop of that infamous sect, by Isiphilus, a lame Egyptian who resided in the same house, and last of all by one for whose sake I before recommended your Splendor to cease further enquiry—by your own daughter, Agnella. Farewell.

From Pola,
the 7th of the Kalends.

XXIV

Agnella to her dear Father Anastasius, Priest, Health.

If indeed one like myself may venture to call you Father—if one who has denied all that is her dearest life and hope and comfort, may dare to speak of health.

Read, my Father, that which follows, and then tell me if there can yet be hope or forgiveness for me. For me, who not only have so lately put on the white robe of the salutary laver, but who had only just been counted worthy to eat the Flesh and to drink the Blood of the Immaculate Lamb. Oh, woe is me! Better never to have heard the true faith, better even to have shut my ears to it when preached, than thus to have received it, only that I might deny it. But listen.

This miserable morning, as I was talking to my mother in the women's apartment, where she was spinning, and wondering whether it would ever please Him Who can rule all hearts to open her eyes to the light of His Gospel, Glycerium brought me a message to go to my father by the fish-pond. I went. It was a still morning, of that stillness—for I keep off as long as I can from owning the truth—when summer is just melting away into autumn, and the first leaves begin to fall, and the dew is heavy in the morning. I found him walking up and down, and more discomposed than I have often seen him.

"Agnella," he said sternly, "come here. Did you know that your nurse, Apollonia, died a Christian?"

I felt all my color rush into my face.

"That she died a Christian?"

"Do not repeat my words, but give a plain answer to a plain question. Did you know it?"

Oh, Father, God forgive me! I said faintly, "No."

"You did not?"

"No," I said, now more boldly.

"You are sure?"

"Quite sure."

"My child,"—and he looked very steadily at me—"you paid more than one visit to this woman. Did you not see any others with her?"

Oh, my Father! And so, having denied God, I next denied you.

"No."

"Never?"

"No, I never saw any but my poor nurse."

Then his face brightened up, and he spoke more gently: "It is a weight off my mind. I did not think you could have deceived me. But if ever—if ever—you were led to listen to that cursed sect, I would pray the immortal gods to pour out their utmost vengeance on you and your seducers, one and all alike. But it never will be so, will it?"

And again I said, "Never."

Now, my Father, tell me, and tell me at once—is there hope? I will do everything you desire. If you would have me go to my father at once, and where I denied Christ there to confess Him, I promise you to obey. Only let me hear that there is some kind of hope, that I have not lost all. Tell me what I must suffer, and if my sufferings will suffice, oh, how gladly and thankfully will I embrace them! Farewell.

From Pola,
the 6th of the Kalends.

XXV

*Anastasius, Priest, to his daughter Agnella,
Repentance and Love.*

I have received, my daughter, your letter:
with what sorrow and shame He knows
alone Who knows all hearts.

You say justly that for you, so lately cleansed
in the laver of regeneration, so recently
strengthened by the Food of all strength, that
you should so grievously have fallen, and more
than once or twice denied Him Who had so
lovingly called you—this is a grief that I have
scarcely ever before known the like of, never
one so great.

But yet there is hope.

I would not have you now think to atone for
cowardice by presumption. I would not have
you provoke your father to new acts of rage
against Christ by voluntarily confessing Him.
But pray, pray night and day, that this your
sin may be blotted out. And to prayer add such
self-denial as you may do without suspicion.
Especially you might remember that which
David says, "Mine eyes prevent the night-

watches," and rising for some space in the midst of every night, since you have sinned like Peter, to weep like Peter also.

Then, if the trial comes again, the Lord Jesus give you grace, at whatever cost, to confess Him in this world, lest you be denied of Him in the next!

Had your denial been public, you must (when God shall restore peace to the Churches) have been put to public penance. As it was private, your repentance will also be private. Nevertheless, for a certain season I forbid you to draw near the Lord's Table, how long a season must partly depend on the earnestness of your own repentance, and partly on the danger and opportunities of the times.

O my daughter! Earnestly shall I pray for you, but earnestly also must you pray for yourself else Satan, because he has once triumphed, will obtain his second victory more easily—and so shall you bring down my grey hairs with sorrow to the grave. Farewell.

From my appointed place.

XXVI

Agnella to her Father in the Lord, Health.

Oh, dearest Father! You have lifted me up as it were from death to life. How I abhor and loathe and would fain punish myself, God only knows. Pray that I may continue steadfast and increase more and more in my repentance, and that I may stand firm when the danger shall be.

My father has even now given notice that in a few days, our house is to be ready for the reception of the Augustus—who comes (it seems) to enquire into the number of the Christians here. Once more, pray for me, that if the Lord shall require me to confess His Name before the Emperor, I may do it with joy. Farewell.

From the Palace, hastily,
the 5th of the Kalends.

XXVII

Anastasius, Priest, to his beloved daughter Agnella, Health.

Yet one word, most dear child, now to bid you stand firm. If the Emperor comes, of a verity hell will be loosed against the followers of the Lamb. But, as it is written: "They overcame him by the word of truth, and by the testimony which they held, and they loved not their lives unto the death."

And now, according to the power which the Lord hath given me for edification, not for destruction, and considering the imminent danger to which the coming of the Augustus will expose us all, I free you, most dear child, from all censure of the Church on condition that you still for awhile live the strictest life of penitence that circumstances will allow. Do not at present, except in case of great necessity, seek to see me. If it be necessary, you know where to come,* and how there to

---

Note by a subsequent possessor of the letters. "I have heard that this place was a ruined arbor that stood in the corner where the road to Pisinum separates from that to Parentium. It is now part of a vineyard belonging to Manius Glabro." —JMN

enquire for me. Farewell.

From my place.

XXVIII

Corellia to her dear Agnella, Health.

We are coming, dearest friend, to town. My father has received a summons from the Augustus who, as you probably know, visits Histria.

Greatly do I long to see you again. This that has happened has not altered—and nothing ever will alter—my love. But, truth to say, I must and shall feel strange when first I hold my little darling in my arms.

You shall tell me more than you have done. You shall tell me all that is not forbidden. Thus far I feel certain: that there are no Thyestean feasts, no mysteries of unspeakable iniquity, in a sect where you can be happy and, if I have been—as you once argued yourself—wrong in taxing your religion with those crimes, I may be mistaken about it in other respects.

But then, how can I be certain that at present you know all? You spoke, yourself, of certain other mysteries which needed a preparatory initiation and lustration. If these have not been as yet opened to you, how can we tell what still remains behind? But this and other things I shall shortly hear from your lips themselves, and till then believe in my love, and farewell.

From Pomerium,
the 4th of the Kalends of September.

XXIX

Agnella to her father Anastasius,
Health and Love.

You forbade me (most dear Father) to seek after you without special cause. I think that I now have such a cause.

You know that here are with us my father's friend, with whom I was lately staying— Flaminius Acerra, and his daughter, my beloved Corellia.

As before, so now, Corellia has enquired much about my conversion, and like him of whom you were telling me, even now she says, "Almost thou persuadest me to be a Christian."*

In fine, if you will allow her, she desires to see you. I do not know that it is with the desire of finding a solution of any especial difficulty, for none such, in particular, she appears to me to have on her mind. But she knows how little I can tell her, and I hope that the Lord Himself is leading her more and more into the knowledge of His truth. If you think well to grant her request, it can only be done before the Augustus shall arrive.

And this let me further, my Father, tell you I have been obliged, by an almost necessity, to take my own slave, Glycerium, into my secret. She has been brought up with me from childhood, and I am confident that neither the rack nor the scorpions would tear that secret from her. I believe that she would die for me with joy.

---

*These are the words of King Herod Agrippa II to Saint Paul as recorded in Acts of the Apostles 26:28.

And if you think me imprudent, remember how much more I should have to trust others if I had no confidence in her. Farewell.

XXX

Anastasius, Priest, to Justus, Bishop, Health in the Chief Pastor of Pastors.

Days pass on, most holy Father, bringing fresh and fresh trophies of the Lord's grace. And (unless I am much mistaken) hastening also the time when that grace must be magnified in me, when I stand before the Lion.

Meanwhile, as the word of God prospers and runs mightily, there are, nevertheless, difficulties which perplex me sorely, and on one of these I write to your Paternity word.

Agnella, yet a *candidate* after Baptism, is in a situation of great peril: it being now announced that the Cæsar, in revenge for that Victory which was destroyed, will shortly visit Pola, and will take up his abode in the

Præfectorial Palace, to which the great men of the suburban district are assembling in the city. Among these comes Acerra, once on a time Præfect of Dalmatia, and his daughter Corellia, the latter a dear friend of Agnella.

Yesterday, from these two I received a most perilous visit, for Corellia also desires to give her name to Christ. But I cannot say that I am altogether satisfied with her wishes. Undoubtedly, after a sort, she does wish it. She has genius beyond that of her age and sex. She is manifestly ready to break the shackles of her old superstition and, to a certain degree, she sees the beauty of our faith. But, as it seems to me, her heart is utterly untouched by the Lord's love.

Agnella has many faults—has already had one grievous fall—but her whole heart is on fire with the love of our Lord. That one thing, as we all know, will counterbalance all other drawbacks and will present her hereafter without spot before the throne of God. But in Corellia it is all cold and brilliant, in heavenly things I mean, for that she *can* love, her whole demeanor towards this her dear friend most amply shews. And, as I verily think, she would, need so being, die for her. She demands Baptism. Sufficient knowledge she will soon have, but yet I think that I should do both her and that most blessed laver injustice were I as yet to admit her thereto. The rather, that so heavy a trial is hanging over all of us.

I think, holy Father, that were you here, you would approve of my determination. Let what may happen, I have set it down on paper to the intent that if the case hereafter, when I am taken, should come before you, you may know what were my reasons for deferring a while in this circumstance the salutary washing. Farewell, and remember my flock and myself in all your prayers and sacrifices.

From my accustomed place.

XXXI

Quintus Flaminius Acerra, to his little heart, Caia, Health.

The more I grieve, beloved wife, that the evil blast which fell upon you prevented your accompanying us hither, the more I am bound to set down, so far as I may, whatever shall happen for your amusement and, in good truth, I would give much that you were here. Not so much that all is in preparation for the reception of the Augustus—that beacon-fires are to be lighted all across Histria as soon as he shall make the promontory of Pomerium, that the priests are choosing the victims, and the maidens occupying themselves with garlands. In these things I am too old and, *herclé*, I think the world also is, to take much interest. But there is something in this house which I do not understand and, truth to say, do not overlike. But you shall hear. I am somewhat fevered from the banquet, and the pleasant breezes of this September night, that breathe round me while I write, will send me refreshed to bed.

You may remember the little pine-grove which skirts the hill, immediately behind the Præfectorial Palace. It is, indeed,

> *Nulli penetrabilis astro*
> *Lucus iners.**

---

*From the *Thebiad* of Statius, Book X, translated as: "a dense grove impenetrable by any star."

Two mornings agone, I was walking (for you know it is my custom to rise early) after the bath, and whether chance or a certain divinity directed my steps that way, I mounted the hill and thence cast my eye along the long line of Histrian coast that stretched away even to Pomerium. I stayed so long that I feared to be late for the morning meal and therefore pushed through the wood as the shortest way. There I came upon Agnella, kneeling on the ground and apparently in earnest supplication to the immortal gods. Her arms were stretched to their extreme length, and so great was the fervor of her prayer that my footfall did not disturb her till I was within a few yards of her. Then she started up, seemed for one moment disposed to run off, apparently altered her determination, and came forward to me.

I would have bantered her on thus volunteering for the office of a priest, but I saw that the tears were in her eyes, and I made no allusion to what had passed. So we talked of indifferent matters till we were entering the Præfectorial grounds. Then, as if summoning up a resolution with all her courage, she said, "You came on me just now by accident. I ask you, Flaminius, to keep what you have seen to yourself."

"Surely," said I, "my old friend's daughter might securely ask me something harder with certainty of gaining her request. But tell me, for I have known you, lady, from childhood, if there is anything which I can do for you. You seemed in distress. Could I in any way assist you? I have influence with your father, and would gladly exert it for you."

"I thank you," she said gently but firmly, "but I am not in distress and, except the request I have made, have nothing further to ask. I know, if I had, that I might trust your kindness. But indeed it is not so."

"To you, my Caia, I tell everything and therefore think it no breach of confidence to have repeated this, especially on account of that which follows.

I confess that I imagined this, perhaps, some love affair in which Agnella had been crossed, and Jupiter grant it be so!

That evening the Præfect had ordered abundance of flowers from a certain horticulturist in the suburbs, and both his wife and his slaves and our Corellia set themselves to the task of forming garlands for the animals and for the pedestals, especially of Augustus and of the Eternal Fortune of the Roman empire. I was in the women's apartment—Acilius also.

"Which will you two and Glycerium undertake?" asked the mother.

"Which shall it be, Agnella?" enquired our daughter.

"I have something else to do," said Agnella, hastily. "Take which you like, but do not wait for me." And she left the room.

"That poor girl gets worse and worse," said the mother. "None used to be so fond of garlanding the temples as was she, and now I cannot get her to take the least interest in such matters."

"She looks to me," said I, "much better than when she was at Pomerium."

"She does," replied Terentia, "and she is. Her appetite is better, and our freedman the physician thinks her stronger. But I will not have her thus stay by herself. Go, Glycerium, and desire her to come to me."

Glycerium went and presently Agnella came.

"Did you send for me, mother?"

"Surely. I want you to be yourself again and to help us. Look at these roses—a pity they will fade so soon—but for two days they will look well."

"Where are they to go?"

"As a wreath, I think, for the head of Eternal Rome."

She took them up listlessly, and played with them. Then presently, "The Emperor's chair of state, will not that also be decked?"

"Yes. Would you like that task better?"

"I think I should." And she set to work.

"Ah, my darling," cried her father (you know how fond of her he is), "so you, too, are like the rest of this degenerate age and care nothing for the worship of the gods!"

He was not looking at her as he spoke, but I was. Cheek, neck, shoulder, perfectly burnt with the blush that his words called up, and at the same moment a most frightful thought darted into my mind. Since this, I have confirmed it by many accidental pieces of testimony, worthless each in itself but when taken together, carrying conviction to me.

I feel confident that this poor girl has been seduced by the Christian superstition.

Now, if this be so, though I hardly think that even one so zealous as is the Augustus for the worship of the immortal gods would dare to touch her life, yet the misery her confession would occasion is not to be told. I would spare her father and mother. I would spare all.

And therefore, at this time, I desire your advice. You must believe me when I say that from divers incidents too long to set down here, I am persuaded that my first suspicion is true. Would you have me, then, speak in private to the poor creature, and offer her, from you, a home at Pomerium while the Augustus is at Pola? We could keep her secret. It would be enough to her father—who yields to every whim of hers—that she asks for quiet and that you should say how, in your present health, a quiet companion is the very thing you desire. To us alone the matter will be known, and how can we tell but that we may open her eyes to the filthy practices of these brutish men? I send the slave Stilicho with this, in order that I may at once receive an answer, for no time is to be lost. Farewell.

*From the Præfectorial Palace at Pola,
the Kalends of September.*

XXXII

Caia to her most beloved Husband, Health.

Whatever seems best to you, dearest husband, is approved by me. I pity her if it be as you imagine, but the immortal gods send better things. I am now again well. Farewell.

Very hastily,
from Pomerium.

XXXIII

Agnella to her more than Father,
Health always.

The great God and our Savior be praised, dearest Father, that I may have recourse to you in troubles! For indeed I am sorely perplexed. I had seen for some time that my father's friend Flaminius observed me closely, and though he said no syllable to Corellia, I feared he suspected more than any other. Yet he is so kind, so true, so good. He has lived in such perfect love and union with his wife and is so generous a master to his servants, that I have prayed again and again that he may find mercy of the Lord in that day.

The other day he came upon me in my favorite pine-wood while I was in prayer. I asked him not to mention what he had seen, and he kept his promise. From that time I have imagined that he has been trying to find out my secret and I have been right.

I was this afternoon standing by the tank in our garden and feeding the fish. Corellia had gone with the rest to the temple. Suddenly I heard a step on the garden walk and Flaminius Acerra was by me.

"So you are not at the temple?" said he.

"You see I am not."

"And is it wrong to ask why not?" he returned.

I smiled and said: "Would not my fish give you a sufficient answer?"

"Well," he replied, "this time perhaps they might," and he began to speak of their beauty. But still I felt something more was coming. At last—

"You do not often, I think, go to the temple?"

"I have not been often since you were here."

"Nor lately?"

"Nor lately."

"Nor worked garlands for the immortal gods?"

I made no answer.

"Nor, as I think, eaten viands consecrated to them?"

Still I was silent.

After a pause—"Agnella," he said, "you are a Christian."

I felt my heart give one leap, as if it would beat no more: but I was resolved not again to deny Him Whom I love best.

"I am."

Then he spoke most kindly. He said that he was not one of those who were for persecuting any sect: that, very probably, all had some truth in them, that whatever he had in times past done against Christians, he had done simply as bearing office in the republic and bound to obey its laws. He shewed me the danger I should now run: the grief and misery if the Augustus should discover my secret in which my poor father and mother would be plunged, and he besought me to pay a visit to his wife at Pomerium while the Emperor is here. He would make any excuse to my father—none shall know the true reason but himself and his Caia from whom, he said, he had no secrets.

And now, my Father, what do you advise?

All he says is true. I shall be in danger if I stay. But I have denied my faith to my father once. Ought I not boldly to confess it now? If I had none to consult, I should stay. If you tell me to go, I shall go. I have promised him my answer tomorrow. If I go, I will tell Corellia that he knows all. It may spare her trouble.

Only this I would pray you remember: even if it were right for another, in my place, to avoid the danger, ought not my former sins to compel me to stay? Tell me that you have not forgotten this, whatever your resolve, and I am ready to obey. Farewell.

From Pola,
the 3rd of the Nones.

XXXIV

Anastasius, Priest, to his beloved Daughter,
Health and peace.

O̲ur Lord hath said, my daughter, "When they persecute you in one city, flee ye to another," and albeit it has always been held that His priests and other of His chosen servants are not bound to this law, yet for such as you there can be no doubt. It is not by presumption you must efface the memory of cowardice. Go, then, and the Shepherd of the lambs be now and evermore with His tender little lamb! Go, and (since we shall scarcely meet in this world again, if the Emperor begins a local persecution here) may He grant both you and me to live unto Him or to die unto Him, that living and dying we may be evermore and only His own. Farewell.

From my place.

XXXV

Quintus Flaminius Acerra to his Caia,
Health.

It is, my heart, as I expected. And, seeing such reports are not very safe for ink and paper, I will leave to tell you of how I made my discovery till after I shall see you myself, or she to whom it refers shall think fit to see you. She would not at once consent, though thanking me most heartily for my proposal, and said that she must first take counsel. In a few hours she sought me again, and said that if I would arrange the matter with her father, she would go with joy.

With him I had no great difficulty. I spoke of the wearisomeness and bustle of the Emperor's arrival: that however much other girls were taken with such pomp, Agnella was none of them. I talked of the visit as a kindness to you, and said that you had always been fond of the child. And so, finally, since he cares more for the health of his daughter than for aught else, I persuaded him. Her mother was less pleased: spoke of the sacrifices they had uselessly offered, of her going before, of the necessity that she should be presented to the Augustus. But Dolabella stood firm. In brief, she will leave this place with Agathodorus tomorrow. I despatch Sosias therefore overnight. Receive her as if she were not guilty of this folly, so will you be more likely to release her from it. Farewell.

From the Præfectorial Palace,
the 3rd of the Nones of September.

XXXVI

Corellia to her Agnella, Health.

You have been gone but three days, dearest, and it already seems as if I had lost you for a year. You shall hear at length all that has happened. Only, as four months ago you craved my forgiveness if I should be vexed or annoyed at that which you told me, so must I now do to you, as you shall presently hear.

Well, the Augustus has come. The day before yesterday from the early morning he was expected, and gradually from the sea-coast and from the inland, multitudes assembled on the quay and along the beach. Hundreds ascended the amphitheater and stood fearlessly on the outside of the highest arches, for in that sway and hand-to-hand push of the crowd, one might easily have been swept over the marble side. My father and yours and the ædile of the city and the Chief Augur and others, with the Flamen of Jupiter, assembled at the little pier where the Emperor was to land, and where a temporary altar had been erected. A ram was led thither garlanded, for sacrifice was to be done to Neptune.

At length round the point, we saw the sails of the imperial galley, for the wind was very fair. Then we heard the music of pipes and hautboys, then the dash of the long oars. The vessel was brought to. A plank was shot across to it from the quay, and everybody after this novel fashion prostrating themselves, the Augustus stepped on shore. Then stopping by the altar: "Rise," he said, "citizens. It were well done at all times, it is better done now in this age, when so many miscreants deny the existence and spurn the worship of the immortal gods, that this city should welcome me with a sacrifice. Let us first address ourselves to that. Only thus much and in the presence of the altar itself, I vow: that if any of these blasphemers can be discovered while I am in this town, as I can offer no sweeter oblation to the Olympian deities, so none can be brought more acceptable to me than such."

Agnella, I looked at my father, for I was sure that he was thinking of you, as how should he not be? Oh, how terrible was the Augustus, even in his calmness! What would it be to meet him in his anger? While that sacrifice was going on—I know you will hate me, but you would sooner or later discover it, even did I not tell you now—I made up my mind to acquaint him with all. Your priest said truly, "Your heart is not in your faith." I felt for the moment a desire to be enrolled among those who profess so beautiful a—belief shall I call it? Or fancy? If the world were Christian, as you say it will be, I would readily be Christian too. But I cannot make up my mind to the perpetual fear and concealment and danger, and I know that at the first touch of the *scorpions* my courage would evaporate. I must believe as I can.

Perhaps the One Supreme God will accept me, if I worship Him under the forms of Grecian or Roman art, as well as He will you. Perhaps the times may alter. Only I then determined that as I could do you no harm by confessing the truth, I would tell all to my father that he may shield me in case any awkward investigations or perquisitions should be made. Oh me! That Augustus has a terrible face!

The sacrifice went off well. The augur spoke favorably of the omens, promising the Emperor a great success in this place, the liver being so large and so full of blood. Then we all returned to the Præfectorial Palace where the Emperor was to banquet with the chief men of the city. Six stibadia were set out. Terentia lay at that of the Augustus. So did my father. I thought not to have been present at all, but the Emperor, finding that you were absent, commanded my presence.

At first there was little conversation. He told of his voyage. He asked about the harbor of Pola, its population, its temples, and by degrees the talk turned to the Christian faith.

"And what discoveries did you make," enquired the Augustus, "on investigating the sacrilege of which we wrote to you?"

"Three miscreants suffered for it," your father replied.

"That was well," answered the Emperor, "but thirty times three, had there been so many of these vermin, would ill have satisfied the just wrath of the gods. Was the priest among them?"

"He was not, Lord."

"Had he then paid the penalty of his crimes previously?"

"Unhappily, no, Lord. But it is said that he is at Tergeste or Aquileia."

"He must be procured," said the Emperor. "Before I sleep this evening, let orders be given on the subject. Or, I will give them myself. Who is the chief officer of your police?"

"He is called Pythodorus, Lord."

"In Pola, now?"

"He was on the quay today, Sire, and is presently about the palace."

"It is well. Let him then be commanded to present himself to me at the second hour of the evening. Enough of that at present."

Then he turned the conversation to other subjects. But oh, my Agnella, what a tumult of fear was I in all the dinner! If your priest should be discovered! If your own change should become known! In what horrible danger do you both stand! Think as hardly of me as you will for what you will call my levity, my fickleness, my changeableness, but believe that I do love you still and whatever else I cannot believe in, I believe in you.

As soon as ever I could see my father alone, I told him all. I said that I had been sorely tempted to give my name to Christ. I only did not tell him that I had seen your Priest, for that secret I feel bound to keep and even to deny it, if I should be taxed with such a charge. My father looked graver than ever I have seen him look, but he was very kind. But he told me if any question should arise concerning these matters before the Emperor, to confess the whole truth, and then the worst that could happen would be that I should be ordered to sacrifice—which Jove knows I would gladly do—whereas any prevarication would be my ruin.

He also told me that Pythodorus had seen the Emperor and had been ordered to wait on him again tomorrow.

He has a necessity to send for certain papers

at Pomerium and by his messenger I forward this. Write, if you can, by the same.

From the Præfectorial Palace,
the 8th of the Ides.

XXXVII

Pythodorus to Diocletian, Emperor, pious,
pacific, victor, ever Augustus, Health.

K nowing, Lord, your earnest desire to receive the best and fullest tidings regarding the manumitted slave of the Præfect, Apollonia, who died in the Christian faith, I would most humbly entreat that the Præfect himself be not present when you are pleased to interrogate me further thereupon. The reason is not for a written communication, but will at once, Lord, seem good to yourself and to any counsellors whom you shall select to hear me with yourself. Farewell.

From Pola,
the 8th of the Ides of September.

XXXVIII

Agnella to her (yet not her) Corellia, Health.

Y ou thought rightly—you, whom I must still call dearest. Never have I yet felt such sorrow as when I read your letter. I had thought the Priest harsh in refusing your wish. Now I only see his wisdom and his true kindness. If this were to be so, then thank God that you are not baptized. You tell me of my danger, and there may be something in it. But I cannot even think of it when I remember what you might have been and what you are. O my more than sister! How earnestly I pray, and shall continue to pray to the last, that God may still touch your heart, so that all pain, all danger, may seem less than nothing compared with the one joy of being His to Whom I have given myself, and to Whom you were so nearly giving yourself!

As for other matters, your mother is kindness itself. The moment we were left alone she took me in her arms, caressed me, wept a little, and said: "Be what you will, my dear child, and you will have no reproach or harsh language from an old woman like me. Only, for your dear father's and mother's sake, do not run into danger—I might say for our sakes too, and may the gods preserve you!"

Your messenger is in great speed to return, so I again say, Farewell.

From Pomerium,
the 7th of the Ides of September.

XXXIX

Quintus Flaminius Acerra to his Caia,
Health.

Events and dangers so quickly follow each other, that I hardly know where to begin.

Yester-evening our daughter confessed that she too had nearly been led away by this cursed superstition. But about her I have no fear, and more of that when we meet.

This morning, after the Augustus had left the bath, he desired to see me alone. When I had gone to him, after salutation made— "Read this," he said, " and tell me what you think of it."

It was a letter from Pythodorus which he gave me, and I enclose.*

In my heart I knew well what it meant, but what advice to give on the matter I knew not, whether it were better that Dolabella should be present at the accusation against his own daughter, or whether for her it would be safer that he should be absent. I paused so long that the Augustus said, rather irritably, "Well, it matters not what you think. I have resolved to do what this Pythodorus, who seemed to me last night a sensible man, requests. And I shall require your presence."

I bowed, and only added, "When, Lord?"

"At the sixth hour. I have already obtained information of one Isiphilus, an Egyptian by birth but a Christian, who is said to be hiding at Parentiolum. It is between here and Pomerium, is it not?"

"At an equal distance from both, Lord, but not on the direct road thither."

"I have, therefore, requested the Præfect

---

*This was, of course, the letter marked XXXVII. in the present collection. —JMN

himself to superintend the arrest of this wretch and to bring him before me, and he will start presently. As soon as he is gone I shall request your presence at this examination."

Accordingly, at the sixth hour I again waited on the Augustus in the little banqueting-room, that which looks out over the Adriatic. Besides myself, Syagrius only, his private secretary, was in attendance. Pythodorus was introduced, and a quaternion of guards stood without the door.

"You wished to speak to me without the presence of the Præfect. It is a somewhat unusual request, but I have heard that you are an active and trustworthy officer. What have you to tell me?"

"Your Splendor was last night enquiring about the death of the manumitted slave, Apollonia."

"We were."

"And of those who attended it."

"True."

"I thought, Sire, it might be more agreeable to you to hear in the Præfect's absence that his daughter was one."

"What!" turning to me—"Agnella?"

"He has no other daughter, Lord," I said.

Diocletian's brow darkened.

"Did you tell the Præfect this?"

"Lord, I did."

"When and how?"

"Lord, in that letter,"* and Pythodorus handed one to Syagrius.

"And what said the Præfect?"

"Lord, he was frightfully agitated. But he afterwards saw his daughter alone. She confessed that she had been there, but denied that she knew the woman to have been a Christian."

"And how knew you that she *was* aware of that?"

"Lord, on one of her visits there, there was a Christian priest who goes by the name of Anastasius, and she is now a Christian herself."

Diocletian's wrath was frightful. "Ha!" he said, "is this all a deception? Flaminius, she is at your house. What did you know of this?"

"Nothing, Lord," I said as calmly as I could, "but that the young lady who is a dear friend

---

*That, doubtless, marked XXIII. in the present collection. —JMN

of ours seemed ill, and quiet was expressly recommended by the physicians. My wife, who is also ill, was glad of her company, and they are there together now."

"What evidence have you that this girl has joined that sect?"—to Pythodorus.

"Lord, she met the priest at the house where Apollonia used to live and there settled with him to be baptized."

"Your witness?"

"I can produce him, Lord, he is in the city. It is a boy, named Æmilianus, whom I employ to search out offenders."

"It is not worth while," said the Emperor after some thought. "It will be necessary that Agnella herself should be forthcoming and I give you in charge to fetch her, but not till tomorrow. I will have her father at home first. In the meantime, Flaminius, all that has passed here is a secret."

I said that it should be and my Caia knows how I have kept my word.

But further, I have despatched Agathodorus, who may be trusted, to his master with the news, in order that Acilius may take what steps he likes. I am sure that if Agnella remains firm, her father's rank and favor will not save her life. The Augustus has since said, "Were it my own daughter, if she worshipped Christ Jesus the Crucified, she should die."

I dare not do more than I have done. Warn Agnella of her danger, but tell her that I cannot preserve her. She must look to her own safety.

These are troublous times, my Caia. Farewell.

From the Præfectorial Palace,
the 8th of the Ides of September.

XL

Agnella to her Father, that which God willeth.

To you, my now only Father, I write what will, in all likelihood, be my last letter. If it be, this believe: that I have laid up my whole future in God's care, and that I have everyday and every hour those dearest words in my heart—how dear He only knoweth of Whom they speak: "οἶδα γὰρ ᾧ πεπίστευκα καὶ πέπεισμαι ὅτι δυνατός ἐστι τὴν παραθήκην μου φυλάξαι εἰς ἐκείνην τὴν ἡμέραν."*

You heard that I was coming here. Nor have I time now to relate how kindly I was received by Caia, and what two happy days I spent here.

Then came the sad tidings of my Corellia's apostasy.

Then came a letter written in great haste by Flaminius to his wife, that the Augustus had been informed by the police—how they discovered it I know not—of my giving my name to Christ, and was about to command my presence at Pola, where (said he) it would go hard with my life notwithstanding my father's favor with the Emperors. He had also written to my father, then at Parentiolum, despatched thither by the Emperor to apprehend Isiphilus, in order that he might take any steps regarding me he thought best.

My father came this morning early in the twilight before I was up. I did but merely throw on a palla, and then he entered.

He asked me if it were true.

---

*The English of the text is: "I know whom I have believed, and am persuaded that He is able to keep that which I have committed unto Him against that day." 2 Timothy 1:12. —JMN

I said, "Yes."

He asked, "What did you tell me before?"

I said with many tears that I had been guilty of a falsehood—a gross, wicked falsehood—a falsehood I never could forgive myself for, and that nothing but infinite mercy could forgive.

Coming up close to me he said, exceeding calmly, "Then you are a Christian?"

"Yes, I am."

Oh, how shall I tell you, my Father? How can I bear to write it? I had loved him so much, I had been his pet from childhood. He had been so kind, so loving: everyday and hour had joined us together more closely, and now—

He struck me. Partly from the blow, partly from grief, I fell on my knees before the couch.

"Listen," he said. "Flaminius thought I would move heaven and earth to save you. I would not walk across the room if your life depended on it. You have disgraced a family that has been stainless since the days of Cannae. And if there be any Erinnyes may they—"

"Oh, no, my father! For love's sake, no!"

"If there be any Erinnyes, to them I commit

you here and hereafter, you and all that believe in that—"

But I cannot write what he said of my Lord and my God.

"One petition I will make of the Augustus, and he will grant it. I will ask an employment that may take me and your mother from Pola, while he does what he will with you."

I begged, I conjured him, to let me have one, only one, gentle word—to say but that he pitied me, to believe that I loved him.

He had struck me, and he cursed me, and so he left me.

Then came Caia, O so gently and lovingly! She said that she knew not how to speak to me, what comfort to give me, and she did not. But yet her kindness was so sweet.

"My husband," she said, "tells me in this letter that he cannot do more for you, but I am sure he means me to help you. Let us take counsel how you may best fly."

O my Father, was I wrong? I said I would fly no more. After my father's curse it seems as though I had no home on earth, and besides, I will not involve these kind friends in my destruction. I do not think that I am wrong.

It is no presumptuous confidence in my own strength, but I trust in Him Who is all power. We are now hourly expecting the messenger who is to conduct me to the Augustus, and Caia, in her motherly kindness, goes with me.

Farewell, O my Father to whom I owe every hope, all the trust I have! Farewell! And pray that, living or dying, I may be the Lord's.

From Pomerium,
the 7th of the Ides of September.

XLI

Marcus Acilius Dolabella, Præfect of Histria,
to Diocletian, Emperor, Health.

You have heard, Lord, of my daughter's infamy and my own distress.

I would make no petition for her—better she die as a malefactor than live as a Christian.

But if former service has merit with the Augustus, I would crave, resigning the Præfecture of Histria, for instant employment in a distant province, whither I may at once, with my unhappy wife, depart. Farewell.

From Parentiolum,
the 7th of the Ides of September.

XLII

Diocletian, Emperor,
to Marcus Acilius Dolabella, Health.

I have received, my Acilius, your letter, and I join my grief to yours. I relieve you of the charge of the Histrian Præfecture.

And willing to give a proof of my undiminished—my increased—love to one who thus reverences the immortal gods, as for their sake to resign an unworthy and degenerate daughter, I hereby raise you to the charge, just vacant, of Augustal Præfect.

You will depart within two days to your new office and during that time your daughter shall be kept a prisoner at Pomerium. Farewell.

From Pola,
the 7th of the Ides of September.

XLIII

Quintus Flaminius Acerra, Præfect of Histria, to his Caia, Health.

You will wonder, my Caia, at these new honors. Would to Jove I had them not!

What has passed at Pomerium I have not yet heard. But yesterday, Dolabella returned insane, as it appeared to me, rather than in his senses. He had already by letter besought the Augustus to relieve him of his Præfectal cure and to give him employment at a distance, surrendering his daughter to whatever fate the Emperor should think good. He instantly received the Augustal Præfecture, which happens to be vacant, and an injunction to depart at once to its charge and management.

I instantly went to him and conjured him by all that I thought would bind him to intercede for his daughter. No, he was firm. He would have no Christian vipers in his family. I represented her to him, exposed in the arena to the insults and jeers of the whole city population—a maiden like herself, never yet subjected to rougher handling than the embrace of a father, a mother, or maiden friend—torn with the scourge or stretched on the Little Horse or exposed on the Cross. I conjured him, if he would not intercede for her life, at least to pray that her sentence of death might be mild. Not even so could I induce him. He would not allow me to see his wife—what her feelings are I can only imagine. He takes her with him this very night on their way to Tergeste, or Capris,* whence they sail for Alexandria.

Finally, I left him an open enemy. "If you," said I, "suffer that tender child, that lovely daughter, to be made a spectacle in the arena without one effort to save her, your name should descend with the Medeæ or Thyestæ of old. Little as I can expect from my own exertions, I will try all they can do. I am a true worshipper of the immortal and most blessed gods. But sure I am that their devotion will not be increased by such cruel justice, or rather injustice, as you propose."

Hence, my Caia, I went to the Augustus.

Capris: Renamed Justinopolis in the 7th century AD, and later Capo d'Istria, it is now Kopar in modern-day Slovenia.

In brief, I utterly failed.

"Let the girl sacrifice," he repeated over and over again, "and not a hair of her head shall be touched. Let her refuse, and I will still give her a chance—that of prolonged punishment. I will not cut her off in her obstinacy. A little sharp pain and an obstinate girl will easily be brought to her senses." And he then appointed me Præfect in the place of Dolabella.

I thought of the possible exposure of Agnella in the theater, and that my duty would take me there and resolved to decline.

"Most generous Lord," said I, "I know not how to express my thanks for—"*

. . . . . .

. . . to do what I could, not what I would.

I cannot but trust, however, that even yet the girl, who wants not for sense, may come to a sane mind. This only disturbs me, that all through these troubles women have

---

*Here, unhappily, the manuscript is imperfect, one whole leaf missing.The fragment shews that Acerra must have expressed his views with some boldness. For the classical reader we give the hiatus in the original:
"*Domine benigmissime, inquam, gratias nequeo agere pro tantis in me. . . . . . quod potui, non quod volui, facere.*" —JMN

shewn greater firmness as they call it, greater obstinacy I should term it, than men. But try, my Caia, what you yourself can do. Try if you can by representing to her, her mother's grief, our sorrow, the vexation and disappointment of all her friends, to lead her to a better mind. And remember this, that the time is short.

The arrangements which will be necessary for our change of habitation we will settle together, for I shall be glad of your arrival here as soon as conveniently may be, and the sooner the better. Farewell.

From Pola,
the 3rd of the Ides of September.

XLIV

Agnella, to her Father, Health.

I neither have heard from you, nor perhaps could have heard (most sweet Father in Christ), since my last epistle. Yet as long as I can, I will write. On the morning of the day after I wrote, Pythodorus arrived.

His business was to conduct me at once to the Augustus. Caia insisted on going with me, and my faithful Glycerium.

Both Caia and I were carried in litters, and then, my Father, I for the first time began to learn how every law of courtesy and ordinary decency is violated towards us who follow Christ. Caia was borne in front, and with every treatment that befitted her age and sex and rank. I was borne last and Pythodorus rode by me.

It is not easy to express in words, what yet I felt every moment, how he treated me as one who was beyond the pale of society: how he laughed and joked and uttered jests which, to my father's daughter a month ago, it would have been worth his place to have vented. And how once, when he recited to me those lines of Horace, —

> — *Tu, nisi ventis*
> *Debes ludibrium, cave* — *

he so laid his hand on my shoulder, that I was

English translation: "You, if you wish not to be a plaything of the winds, beware."

well nigh calling for assistance, both against his impertinent action and the leer of his wicked eye.

But when we stopped to rest, I besought Caia to keep near me in the journey, and she agreed. And from Pythodorus I suffered no more.

When we reached Pola we were conducted straight to the Præfectorial Palace and were met in the portico by Flaminius, who I now learn is Præfect, my father being Augustal. O God, what do all these things mean?

He received me kindly but gravely, told me that my room was prepared—my old chamber, that Glycerium would attend me there, but that I should not be permitted to leave it till I had seen the Augustus himself—more especially that Corellia would not be allowed to come to me. He conducted me to my chamber and then, the tears in his eyes, said, "My child, if you continue in this obstinacy, you will bring down my grey hairs with sorrow to the grave."

I know nothing further.

I will entrust this letter to Glycerium. She, if anyhow she can, will convey it to you, whom I pray that it may reach, if it be God's will.

And if not, then God's will be done also. Only continue to pray for me. Farewell.

From my chamber in the Præfectorial Palace, Prid. Id. September.

XLV

Corellia to Agnella, Health.

I may not see you, they tell me, but I may write.

O my Agnella, do not deceive yourself! If you persist in your new creed, nothing can save you. I have heard the Augustus himself declare that he will make an example of you.

Think what that means.

You say others have suffered. Yes, my darling. But few, very few, so tenderly brought up, so delicately nurtured, so loved, so watched over as you. Think of the pain, and if that does not convince you, think of the shame. Think of what I cannot, in maidenly words, set down but which will as surely come to pass as I am now writing to you.

You have asked me, "Can those gods be holy and pure who delight in the rites of which we know?" Might I not ask you, "Can He be a true Lover of His own, of their purity, of their modesty, who (being omnipotent, as you say) permits them to undergo the horrible shame of that exposure in the theater?"

You have seen, I know, the Little Horse. My own darling, *could* we either of us bear it? Try *now* to realize your weakness, now while there is time. I blame you not for falling. I fell. But, sweetest pet, do, *do* return!

I would not speak in my own praise, but may I not say thus far? Have I not, to your knowledge, tried from my youth to lead that kind of life which (you say) the gods approve? If among the immortals there is any remembrance of piety, would they have allowed me to make that fatal mistake you say I have done? Surely not—surely not.

Pity me, sweetest one. The Augustus has heard, somehow, that I once was inclined to your faith. He not only made me throw on, in his presence, the sacrificial incense, but told me that if my old companion (you, my lamb) were in the arena, I, to shew my penitence, must be in the state-seats.

What can I say—what can I beseech about this? This: believe what you will, only sacrifice. Granting all you say to be true, then it is true that your God is merciful, then He will forgive. Can you deny this? If you are right, you may sacrifice with impunity. If you are wrong (as I now believe) oh, immortal gods!—

I can scarcely say, Farewell.

Prid. Id. Sept.

XLVI

Agnella to her beloved Father, Health.

O nce more, dear Father, and for the last time.

I have been before the Augustus.

In that very room where I have so often mixed with those who held my father and mother and me as their child in honor, there now I was exposed to every foul interrogation, every mark and token of disgrace.

There were present the Augustus and

Pythodorus and Acerra and the Emperor's private secretary, Syagrius, and one or two others.

The Augustus interrogated me.

"Are you a Christian? For how long? Who converted you?"

I mentioned my nurse.

"What other Christian do you know?"

I declined to answer and then, O my Father! the Augustus commanded Pythodorus to strike me—me a Roman maiden—me the daughter of the Præfect, Acerra not interfering—in the face.

"Had I thought of the consequences?"

I should have one day with bread and water to think of them, and that in the prison. After that, I should meet the Augustus in the theater.

They came presently to fetch me to the prison.

From the Prison at Pola,
the Ides of September.

XLVII

Anastasius to Agnella, Health.

Perhaps a bribe may introduce this.
Only, beloved daughter, stand firm.

If the Lord of heaven and earth were smitten on the Face, shall the daughter of a Roman Præfect complain?

Rely on this: all the Christians in this place are earnest in prayer tonight for you: none of us can forget you, and the God Who Himself suffered, He will remember you, for He has engraven you (and my child knoweth how) on the palms of His Hands.

Hold out, whatever happens! Hold out, whoever be the adversary! Hold out, and see what God's grace can do! Would that I myself were to confess with you! God be evermore with you!

From my place.

XLVIII

Isiphilus to Anastasius, Health.

Taking my life in my hand, I have learnt all I can.

They report her miserably cast down.

They lay ten to one that she will yield.

I have seen Glycerium. She believes it true.

You will judge what you ought to do or whether anything can be done.

The seventh hour of the night,
the Ides of September.

XLIX

Anastasius, Priest, to Justus, Bishop:
to rejoice always in the Lord.

The whole city rings, holy Father, with her victory. What say I, the city? Throughout Histria itself they talk of nothing else. Satan gathered together all his powers, only to the end that they might more illustriously be overthrown. Satan's chief minister came: that Emperor who is drunk with the blood of the saints, came full of vaunting that, this time at least, he would not fail, came and looked on at the arena, and behold, as of old time, "The Lord has chosen new wars." Behold, as of old time, "The Lord hath sold Sisera into the hand of a woman."

The games had been fixed for the third hour, but late on the preceding evening I learnt that they were postponed till noon, when the Emperor himself would take his seat. Then we were told that Agnella, from whom I had heard and to whom I had written in the forenoon, was now confined by herself—that none, not even Glycerium, could have access to her and none could say how she was bearing up.

At the seventh hour, as I and three others were earnest in prayer, we heard a faint noise at the outer door. He that was least known went out to reconnoitre. A boy then, seeing one coming, left an epistle and fled. It was from Isiphilus. He told me that from all he could gather, our poor captive was losing her faith. Hereupon I took counsel with the brethren, for by this time six or seven had met. After some discussion a thought, inspired (I verily believe) by God, darted into my mind. I sent by a safe hand a letter to the police-officer Pythodorus, who has been long in anxious search of me, offering if I might be with Agnella for the last two hours to put myself into their hands. As soon as the Augustus woke (he ever wakes early) his pleasure was taken thereupon. And it was still early when I received a safeguard, sealed with the private seal of Augustus, appointing me to be there by the fourth hour.

On this, all the brethren assembling with me, I consecrated once more the Holy Mysteries and we received the glorious Body and the precious Blood. I reserved one particle, having dipped it in the life-giving Blood, in the silver box for Agnella, and exhorted all the brethren save those in the amphitheater to remain instant in prayer for her, and the Notary of the Church to be earnest and accurate in recording the Acts. After this I bade them all farewell in the Lord with many tears, went back accompanied only by Isiphilus to my house, arranged everything as for a final absence, and then hard on the appointed time I went down to the prison. The gates jarred back on their hinges, and Pythodorus was there.

"You have kept your word," said he, "and we shall keep ours. Go in. She does not know that you are coming."

I went in. It was a small square room lighted by one grated window high up, paved with stone, dull and damp and fearful. She was kneeling or rather almost prostrate on the ground. When the door opened she took no immediate notice, but directly I said, "My child!" she sprang to her feet. She thanked God a thousand times. Indeed, the joy was almost too much for her.

And when I said, "I am to be with you to the last," and when I told her of the unconquerable strength I had brought her, she said, "Now I may indeed take up my *Nunc Dimittis*."

But how lovingly, yet how bravely, with what faith and hope and love she received the Holy Mysteries? What words of mine can tell?

I asked her if she had ever wavered: she paused a little.

Then, never for herself or on her own account, she said, but at the sight of her father—her dear poor father, and in the hearing of a fearful and Erinnyan curse that he poured forth on her—then, for the agony of one moment, she knew not what to say. But since that not at all, not even when she stood before the Augustus. Not even when he said, "Ere long you will supplicate that mercy which you now despise." Her one desire now was that those she left, her father and mother, and Caia who had shown her so much kindness, and "her poor Corellia," and Acerra, might so be brought into the fold as that someday they might all joyously meet again.

"You will soon, my child, be interceding for them before the Throne of God."

"If—if—"

"There is no *if* in God's grace, Agnella."

"But, my Father, there may be in my own weakness. But tell me, is it known by what—how—in what way—I am to—to—"

"To go Home? It is not, my child. Not to me, that is. But long since known to, long since appointed by, Him Who loves you best of all."

Up to this time she had not comprehended the means by which I had obtained leave to visit her. But something now said, I forget what, discovered it—and her gratitude was almost sad. The privilege to me was so much more than the cost. As soon as I had quieted in some degree her expression of thanks, I once more prayed with her, and we had hardly risen again when Pythodorus entered with three or four of his subalterns.

"The prisoners to the amphitheater," said he.

Agnella took hold of my arm—her own was quite firm.

"You will pray for me to the very last?"

"Our Lord Jesus Christ knows that I will."

There was scarcely a passenger in the streets. All, we imagined, were in the amphitheater. Lovely looked the blue Adriatic, as we passed along its shelly coast, lovely the sunny island of Polella,* lovely the creeks and bays of the indented shore and the olive-yards and vineyards that encircle the city and the clear breezy heights that trend down west.

"I could almost feel faint-hearted," whispered Agnella, "when I think of giving up all this light and all this beauty."

"'Truly,'" I quoted, "'the light is sweet, and a

Polella: Later known as Isola Santa Caterina, this island is known today as Otok Sveta Katarina in Croatia. —JMN

pleasant thing it is for the eyes to behold the sun.' But what, my child, of the true Light and the uncreated Sun?"

High above us now rose the snow-white mass of the amphitheater. A few sea-birds were slowly sailing round its upper arches— arches too dazzlingly bright for the eye to dwell on. Everywhere the awnings were up. We were led round the building. Guards were placed—it seemed to me in unusual force—at each of the four square vomitories. Through the vineyards and olive yards we passed, hearing the suppressed hum of a thousand voices within, sometimes the shout of some popular watchword, sometimes a yell from one of the confined beasts.

Agnella now leant more heavily on my arm, but I think it was only because the road was steep.

The strong small door at the side of the eastern vomitory opened.

"Prisoners, enter."

I go first, she follows immediately.

"Pass on," said the voice of some one whom with eyes just fresh from the noontide

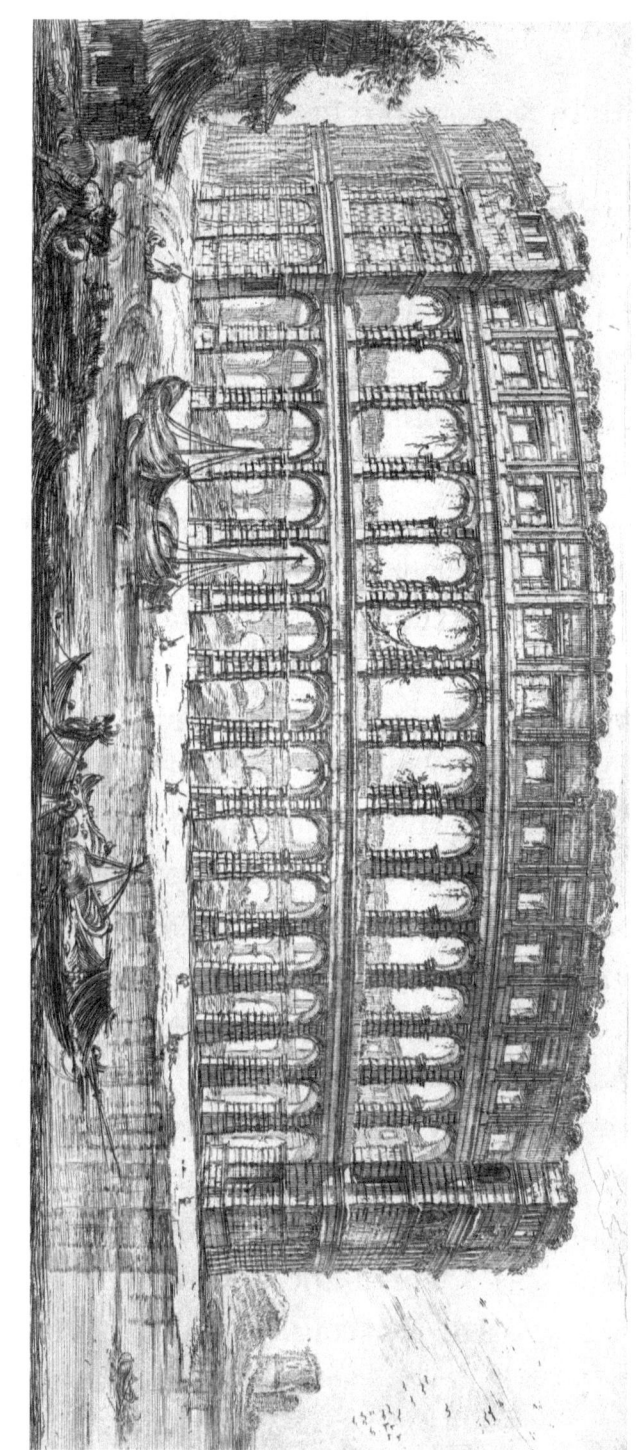

The Amphitheater of Pola as sketched by Giovanni Battista Piranesi, ca. 1748.

brilliancy, we could not distinguish.

Still on through a winding passage. At length we are shewn into a small withdrawing-room, lighted by one taper only. Pythodorus is with us.

"The Emperor commands your instant attendance. Follow."

He opens a door and we forthwith step out on the arena. A surging tumultuous sea of life around. Men rise and lean forward.

"Out with them! Tear them in pieces! Burn them alive! The lions! The lions! A-h-h-h! Jove preserve the Augustus! A-r-r-r!"

Now she trembled painfully. I raised my heart to Him that stood before Pilate.

In the center of the arena was a kind of gibbet set up. It had but one arm. This arm projected some two cubits from the main upright at a height of perhaps five cubits from the ground. From the extremity hung a rope in connection with pulley and pulley-gear, the working tackle being carried along the horizontal beam and so down the upright where was a wheel and handle with holdfast.

As we are led round to the Emperor, we

pass a deep, deadly pool of blood.

"A *meridianus*,"* exclaimed Pythodorus, in reply to my glance.

The Augustus sat in the seat of honor opposite the *cavea*. At his right hand Corellia, on his other side Flaminius Acerra.

"Kneel to the Emperor," said Pythodorus following his own exhortation.

We bowed only.

At the entrance of one of the doors that led from the arena to the vomitory a girl was standing. Agnella looked at her earnestly.

"Oh my Father," (in a low voice) "it is my Glycerium!"

The Emperor speaks.

"When those who should be an example to others of keeping the law, as the members of a Præfect's family ought to be, are the first to break it, few words are best. Lady, do you sacrifice?"

I was astonished that that gentle voice spoke so firmly and distinctly: "No."

Meridianus: Normally, a condemned man forced into gladiatorial combat at the noon-time show.

"Out with the Canidia! Out with the wretch! Burn her! Tear her! Lions! Lions! Fire! Out with her! The Little Horse! A-h-h-h!"

The Emperor waved his hand.

"We ask thrice only, using no solicitation. Do you sacrifice?"

"I have said, Lord.

The howls and yells again.

"Do you sacrifice?"

"I sacrifice not."

"It is my purpose to shew you, Quirites," said then Diocletian, "that in the service of the immortal gods I favor no class of men. This girl, though daughter to one that hath been twice, and that most deservedly, *imperator*—"

"—Your pleasure, sir?" for Acerra seemed to remonstrate, and the Emperor's brow clouded.

"Silence, sir," he presently continued: "though, I say, the daughter to one that has been twice saluted *imperator*, and is a most worthy knight, she has chosen a slave's religion, she shall receive a slave's punishment. Wherefore my pleasure is that she be scourged till she sacrifice or till she die."

While a great shout of exultation went

up from earth to heaven, Glycerium rushed forward and threw herself, in a flood of tears, at her young mistress's feet.

"I knew what it was to be," she sobbed. "They—told—me—this—morning. I have leave—to be with you. I thought it might be—might be a comfort."

"A comfort, my Glycerium? It is indeed. Only—only—someday believe as I do and then we shall be together again."

I saw the notary of the Church of Pola beginning to take down the Acts.

"Not she," cried Pythodorus, "she has too much sense. Come, the people must not be kept waiting." And, laying his hand on her shoulder, he led her towards the gibbet. She held Glycerium's arm and said to me, but only in a whisper, "Oh, if I should fail at last!"

"He will not fail. He cannot fail His own child. 'When thou passest through the waters,' is not that true now? And think, too, what a mighty host of prayers are going up from the brethren here, even at this moment! The martyrs of other persecutions, doubt it not, are here. Your own sweet companions that are to be: Martina, Thecla, Anastasia, and the Son of God Himself, He your own, as you His, is now *standing* for you as of old for Stephen!"

"I *know* He is. 'As in Thee I have trusted, so let me not be confounded.'"

"He That Himself was scourged, can He not sympathize? Will He not help you? Will He not conquer in you? It is His battle, you happy child,"—her eye brightened as I said that— "His, and not yours, that you have to fight."

"Yes, it is."

Two men with masks now came on the arena: the one having six tremendous whips of cowhide, the other, two *scorpions*. The former threw his *scuticae* on the ground, and laid hold of Agnella's *palla*.

"My servant," she said calmly, "will do that."

As she began to be made ready for the sacrifice, I knelt and prayed. Glycerium received her mistress's *palla* and *toga*.

"They are yours, if you like them," said Agnella, quietly.

"Jove destroy me, then," said the man with the *scutica*. "They are my perquisites. She shall have them if she likes to pay, but the work on the *syrma** is worth something."

At this moment the ass with the hooked rope was driven on.

"What is that?" she asked, as Glycerium was unbuckling the *spinther*** that held her *strophium*.

I did not like to answer.

Pythodorus said, "Well, that *is* a droll question. What for, says she? Why, to draw you off when these gentlemen have done with you, that's what it is for."

She turned to me with a sweet smile, her *last* smile, and said, "And was carried by the angels into Abraham's bosom."

But heart cannot conceive, holy Father, what horrible and *praetextate* words, what jeers, what a saturnalia of ruffian and brutal gibes, what gross and filthy insults burst from the rabble of the theater, as Glycerium received from her already half-disrobed mistress first

---

**Syrma:* The trimming at the bottom of the *palla*. "Crispato rigidae crepitant in *syrmate* rugae." *S. Sidon. Apollinar.* xiii. 15. —JMN

***Spinther:* The clasp or buckle of the *strophium*, a kind of petticoat, only much more visible and ornamental. —JMN

the *cyclas*,* and then after a moment's bitter pause in which Agnella looked up earnestly to heaven and her lips moved, the *supparum*. On one hand, ten thousand ministers of Satan, exulting, triumphing, glorying, gloating over their master's work, uttering every loathsome reproach, every foul insult—on the other, one weak girl, in the deepest and cruellest hour of earthly shame, despising it for His sake Who had despised all shame for her.

One of the executioners seized Agnella's hands, squeezing the wrists together as with the force of a vice. The other produced a very small handcuff, set inside with sharp nail-heads. Those wrists, poor child, were slender enough, but this accursed instrument needed a strong man's force ere it would fasten round them, and I saw the grey shade of agony pass for the first time over that sweet face.

"Take courage," I said, "the battle has begun."

"I could not take it, but He gives it to me."

To this handcuff they now made good the tackle from the pulley, and then one of the

---

Cyclas: A kind of under-petticoat. —JMN

executioners held Agnella beneath it, while the other, going behind, turned the handle till he drew up the poor lamb so that she only touched the ground on tiptoe, her weight depending thus almost totally on her strained arms, and her head hanging back. I heard her say over and over again, "Jesus Christ, let me never be confounded." And once, "Jesus Christ, that didst hang on Thy stretched-out arms for me, have mercy!'" And then, as one of the executioners took up a *scutica* in his hands and looked towards the Augustus, she said—and I never knew what prayer meant till I heard the earnest yearning *gasp* of that petition—"O Jesus Christ! O Jesus Christ! Give me patience."

Corellia had hid her face in her hands. I judged that the Emperor commanded her to withdraw them, for she immediately afterwards held them down. He then looked towards the executioner and gave the sign.

The swift cruel hiss of the cowhide, and Agnella had won the first glorious scar of the war. Swung by such a brawny arm, each lash bit deeply and fiercely into so tender a frame, and forthwith that saying of the prophet was fulfilled, "The shield of His mighty men is made red: His valiant men are in scarlet." And still, as if there were strength and healing in the very Name, she cried out, "Jesus Christ! O Jesus Christ! Help me!" And still it also was (told by the firm, cool, matter-of-fact voice of the executioner who was unemployed) "Forty-six—forty-seven—forty-eight—forty-nine—fifty."

"Change," said Pythodorus.

"Time, too," cried the first ruffian. "My arm aches."

"He *is* bringing you through. He is not forsaking you," I said as the other took up a fresh *scutica*.

"He *is*, but in *such* pain as—O pray Him to take me!"

I saw, by the involuntary and half-convulsive motion of the poor mangled frame, the increased agony of a fresh arm and a cowhide unsoftened with blood. She ceased to cry out. I, fearing some device of the Ancient Enemy, began to recite, "And being in an agony, He prayed more earnestly, and His sweat was as it were great drops of blood falling down to the ground."

Then the sweet lamb began again, but with a hoarse and broken voice, "O Jesus Christ! If it be possible! O Jesus Christ, let this cup pass!"

O marvellous grace so manifested! The executioner was again changed, and now the words came gaspingly and pantingly, but lo! they were no longer words of supplication—they were rendering of praise. Even then, when every stroke ate out small fragments of nerve and muscle, with clotted gouttes of blood—even then, when the very bones of the martyr were laid bare—it was "Glory to Thee, Jesus Christ, true God!" And though the sweat of that great agony poured down from her face, yet had that face the look of an angel. Such surely will be those countenances that we shall behold in the Land of the Living.

One loud shriek rang through the amphitheater—I think the martyr heard it not. Corellia had sunk down insensible, and was carried out.

A fifth time was the executioner changed. Then she said, in a low, quivering voice; "It is nearly over. Give thanks for me to the end to Jesus Christ."

I said that hymn, "O Lord, the Only-begotten Son of God," and here and there she yet responded. But when the two hundred and nine-and-thirtieth stroke had been given, there was a convulsive tremor over her whole frame, and the fearful, fearful panting ceased.

"Fainted," said one.

"I don't know that," said the other. "Best get water."

Oh how earnestly I prayed the God of the spirits of all flesh to receive this offering as in full, and not to allow the tortured frame to feel more!

They dashed water over her to no effect. They burnt pungent aromatics under her nostrils—all in vain. Finally, they loosened the rope, and the tabernacle of the now victorious soldier fell heavily to the ground.

Verily they had killed the body. And after that they had no more that they could do.

Instantly two men—I know them both, but think not fit to set down their names—rushed in from the *inter-caveare*,* and each dipped

---

Inter-caveare: The space between each block of wild beasts' dens. —JMN

a hand kerchief in the blood. The mob, awe-struck by the greatness of the Lord's victory, forbare to revile.

And now, holy Father, see how differently God and man judge.

As soon as it was certain that the victorious soul had been set free, the man who yet held the *scutica*, brutally struck the poor head with the reversed handle. Then the ass was brought up; the feet were fastened to the hook, and the body drawn out into the *spoliarium*, tracking the arena with the blood that had been so precious a sacrifice.*

And now, holy Father, I entreat your prayers whether, when this reaches you, I shall still be in the flesh or set free. Immediately after Agnella's triumph I was remanded to prison and have since heard nothing concerning

---

*Anastasius here proceeds to give an account of a miracle wrought by means of the martyrdom of Agnella. Perhaps in an age like the present, it may be omitted, especially as the martyrdom itself is the greatest miracle of all. —JMN

[Modern readers should note that at the time Neale wrote this work (that is, 1861), any hint of the miraculous in a Christian sense was treated with extreme scorn by the British intellectual class—many of whom nevertheless were fond of visiting mediums, spiritists and fortune-tellers.]

myself. These things were done the day before yesterday, but only today have I been able to procure wherewith to write.

Rejoice, therefore, for our most happy and glorious child. And be earnest, I pray you, in intercession and in the Sacrifice for the remnant that are left in this place. Farewell.

From the prison at Pola,
the 16th of the Kalends of October.

L

Quintus Flaminius Acerra, Præfect of Histria,
to Terentia, widow of Marcus Dolabella,
Health.

All has been done, most dear sister in Christ, that we have purposed, and that you have approved.

I have from time to time told you how glorious a church is erecting over the 'Confession' of those constant martyrs of Christ, Saint Anastasius and Saint Agnella. Yesterday, the venerable Bishop of Tergeste having come to us for that purpose, we translated the precious bodies of the martyrs into the Confession, splendid with Istrian marbles and carved with exceeding art.

The vengeance of the impious Diocletian had caused them to be buried in quick-lime, wherefore we could only translate the bones into their new tabernacle. But they shall not be less glorious in the day of the Lord's Second Appearing, now no doubt shortly at hand.

And so the Bishop—now a very aged man—celebrated the Holy Mysteries over the Confession of the martyrs, and then spoke of their felicity. Near them I propose to remove my beloved Caia, trusting myself, in God's good time, to lie by her.

And in a few days we intend to bring my Corellia's first daughter—sons, as you know, she already has–to the salutary laver in the new baptistery where our little Agnella shall be dedicated to God.

And now, my sister in Christ, will you not, seeing that you are a stranger in a strange land and that God, in His supreme wisdom, has not been pleased that you should have laid in a Christian cemetery the remains of your husband (oh that nevertheless he may have found mercy of the Lord!) will you not come and spend your last days with us, who so truly and dearly love you, and where you shall have a mother's interest, as long as you tarry here, in the tomb of Christ's most faithful Virgin and Martyr, Agnella? Farewell.

From the Præfectorial Palace at Pola,
the Nones of May,
Constantine Augustus and Licinius Augustus,
for the third time, Consuls
[May 7, AD 313.]

About the Author

Though little remembered today, **John Mason Neale** (1818-1866) was a 19th century Anglican clergyman. He was a poet, hymnodist, novelist and scholar of the ancient classics. He is perhaps best known for writing or translating the lyrics of several familiar hymns and Christmas carols, including: *Good King Wenceslas*, *Good Christian Men Rejoice*, and *O Come, O Come, Emmanuel*.

Neale was associated with the Oxford Movement of the mid-19th century which sought to re-introduce ancient Church practices into the Church of England. With a keen interest in patristics and as founder of the Sisterhood of Saint Margaret in 1854—a community of Anglican sisters that survives to this day—Neale regularly faced accusations of being too sympathetic to the Catholic Church. In the England of the mid-19th century, such accusations were no small thing, and in Neale's case, criticisms of his leanings sometimes transcended mere verbal barbs from his peers. Indeed, the persecution he and his family endured was lasting and occasionally furious.

His daughter Mary would later write:

> "To us, familiar as we were with his stories of the persecutions of the Church, it perhaps seemed to be the natural lot of a Christian, especially as our parents bore it in a quiet matter-of-fact way. When abusive language was shouted at her outside our window, our mother would pull down the blind and send one of us to practise the piano."*

Anti-Papist hooligans attempted to burn down his home at Sackville College in November of 1848. In a letter, Neale described his family's situation, and also revealed a hint of his bravery in the face of such intimidation: "Anonymous letters are now the order of the day, also pictures of me. This is all part of the same attempt to force us out, but they have mistaken their man. I sometimes really think they will try a bullet before they have done,

---

*This quote and the others in this brief biography may be found in *The Letters of John Mason Neale* (1910) edited by his dauther, Mary Sackville Lawson.

and so murder me..."

In March of 1851, he and his wife were again roughly handled as "agents of popery." Neale's account of the incident, from another of his letters, again gives a sense of his personal courage, as well as that of his wife, Sarah:

> "On a certain Tuesday night a mob of about 150 persons, many of them disguised, paraded the town; that they carried torches, firepans, oil, shavings, straw, and other combustibles; that they disturbed the place with their rough music; that they came up to this College, burnt a bier, a pall, and crosses in our field; smashed many of our windows, the stones being thrown with such force as to indent the wall on the opposite side; lighted a fire against our house, which absolutely melted the lead of one of the windows, and the flame of which was seen above the roof; that the mob retired two or three times, and returned to the assault,

after having had beer in the town; that, when I went out to speak to them, they first attacked me, and had afterwards the cowardice to attack Mrs. Neale; that this took place when my children were, and were known to be, lying seriously ill; and that their illness was very much aggravated by the fear and excitement, and the dense smoke with which the house was filled."

Despite such indignities, John Mason Neale remained an Anglican to his death. Unlike his contemporary, Cardinal Newman, he never swam the Tiber despite his obvious affinity toward Catholic practices.

An immensely prolific writer, Neale scattered numerous little literary gems in his wake which may well be appreciated by modern audiences. Several of these works are set in patristic times, including *The Egyptian Wanderers*, *Exiles of the Cebenna*, *The Quay of the Dioscuri*, and this present volume which we republish with joy.

If you enjoyed this book, you might also be interested in these other high-quality works from Arx Publishing...

Angels in Iron by Nicholas C. Prata
"The novel's principal strength is its attention to historical detail and the unrelenting realism with which the battle scenes—and there are many—are described....In addition to being an exciting action/adventure yarn and quite a page-turner, *Angels in Iron* is valuable as a miniature history lesson....This is a book that belongs on the bookshelf of every Catholic man, should be read by every Catholic boy (11 or older, I would say), and stocked by every Catholic school library."

—*Latin Mass Magazine*

Belisarius: The First Shall Be Last by Paolo A. Belzoni
"Presents and argues for, in an understated way, a Christian way of war, to be waged by manly men who value purity and patriotism for the sake of preserving Christian civilization. *Nobiscum Deus*, they cry in battle. So does this book. Not that the book deliberately carries a political message. On its own terms, it is an ambitious tale, filled with action, spectacle, and intrigues of all kinds"

—John J. Desjarlais, *CatholicFiction.net*

Centurion's Daughter by Justin Swanton
"This was not a book dashed off and rushed to publication but something that had been lovingly labored over....First of all, let me say, I loved it....I strongly recommend this book and would say it is appropriate for young ladies and gentleman 15 years and older and their parents of course. This would be a great Christmas gift, Confirmation gift for your Confirmandi or addition to a High School Curriculum."

—Latin Mass Network

Crown of the World: Knight of the Temple by Nathan Sadasivan
"*Knight of the Temple* is written in a style of historical fiction that was prevalent in American Catholic literature several decades ago and follows in the footsteps of such Catholic classics as *The Outlaws of Ravenhurst* and the novels of Louis de Wohl, but with greater intensity. *Knight of the Temple* is a really excellent work, fraught with tension, that hooks us for part two."

—Phillip D. Campbell III, *Saint Austin Review*

Leave If You Can by Luise Rinser
"Speaking of treasures, I loved *Leave If You Can*. It is a very good book to form people in an understanding of a vocation....People may think that one always is holy and attracted to religion, but that is often enough not the case. One can be called and have an aversion. That's why I think the book has a lot to teach. In that respect, it is a true story."

—Sister Magdalene of the Hearts of Jesus and Mary, OCD

For further information on these titles, or to order, visit:
www.arxpub.com

www.ingramcontent.com/pod-product-compliance
Lightning Source LLC
Chambersburg PA
CBHW050820180626
46814CB00004B/1380